W9-BMP-993

Withdrawn

CRIME IN CORN WEATHER

MARY MEIGS ATWATER

INTERWEAVE PRESS

Withdrawn

Copyright 1992 by Interweave Press

Design/illustration by Susan Strawn
Production by Marc McCoy Owens

 Interweave Press
201 East Fourth Street
Loveland, Colorado 80537

ISBN: 0-934026-84-x
First printing: 3M:1292:BC

PREFACE

Years ago, a friend told me stories she had heard about Mary Meigs Atwater concerning her gun toting, chain smoking, coffee drinking, all-night habits. "You know she wrote murder mysteries, too," she said. Well, I didn't. And I had a hard time squaring the rowdy portrait she painted with what I knew of Atwater's contributions to the literature of American handweaving—the graceful, clear prose, the keen analysis, the traditional patterns, the commitment to beauty and fine craftsmanship.

Recently, in the course of publishing Atwater's autobiography, *Weaving a Life* (Interweave Press, 1992), I developed a fuller picture of this remarkable woman. She was indeed an ingenious and brilliant weaver and an indefatigable teacher. She was also a devoted wife and mother, a sensitive artist, a vocal conservative, a passionate patriot, a fearless adventurer, and an aggressive entrepreneur. She had strong convictions and, yes, some odd personal habits.

One of these was a fascination with the criminal mind, and another was the ability to survive with little sleep. As a result, she frequented the scenes of violent crimes, attended local trials, and wrote "whodunits" and articles for *True Crime* magazine in the wee hours of the morning, after finishing her work for the Shuttle-Craft Guild of American Handweavers.

Crime in Corn Weather is Atwater's only published novel (another exists in manuscript form). Introduced in 1935 both in the U.S. and England, it doesn't fit into either of the major mystery genres of the day—the "tough guy" stories of Dashiell Hammett and Raymond Chandler or the bucolic "cozies" of Agatha Christie and Dorothy Sayer. *Crime in Corn Weather* is as ambiguous and eccentric as its creator. It pokes fun at small-town America, traffics in bad puns and sly jokes, views the natural world with lyrical precision, and takes unconventional, almost whimsical attitudes toward serious social issues.

Crime in Corn Weather has nothing at all to do with weaving, and it has not aged well. But who cares?

Linda Ligon

ACKNOWLEDGEMENTS

We would like to thank Betty Atwater Biehl and Houghton Mifflin for permission to bring this book back into print, and Madelyn Van der Hoogt for her enthusiasm and encouragement.

CHAPTER 1

THE LITTLE TOWN of Keedora sweltered in the heat of midsummer. The sky, bleached of all color, was a white glare; and above the incandescent pavements the air lay in shimmering, glassy planes. There was not enough stirring of the air even to flutter the restless leaves of the cottonwoods, and the tall elms that made a feathery arch over Fifth Street—where all the "best people" lived—seemed too wilted to cast a shade. An inertia of heat-faintness held the place. Dangerous, somehow, full of obscure fermentations, poisonous.

It was smothering, baby-killing, soul-sickening weather. Iowa "corn-weather."

Keedora lay like an island in a sea of corn that lapped at the fringes of the town. Houses that ventured out only a little way beyond the concrete, the iron lampposts, and the clipped lawns were overwhelmed in it—a vast green tide that stood half-roof high like a tidal wave about to break.

The corn exulted in the heat, flourishing its gold-green spray of plumes and spreading its shimmering leaves to the glare. It was busy gathering the sunlight into hard yellow grains, to be transmuted presently into super-fat porkers for the Chicago markets, and an ultimate appearance as crisp rashers of bacon on a million breakfast tables.

The insects, too, loved the heat. In the thickets of sweet clover and rank weeds that bordered the dusty roads and fringed the little river—at this season no more than a network of shallow runnels between thirsty sandbars—a myriad flying and crawling things shrilled happily.

A few automobiles, like overgrown beetles, shuttled back and forth along the concrete highways. At the top of the long grade that sloped down to the river and its red iron spiderweb of bridge a black sedan was drawn up on the shoulder of the road. A man was just finishing changing a tire. He was a middle-aged man of the "prominent citizen" type, tall and spare and gray. It had taken him a long time to change the tire, for his hands were unused to the task; besides, he was much concerned to keep his seemly gray clothes and well-shined shoes from the grease and dust. He need not have worried; his clothes would soon be stained with something far more dreadful than grease—and he would not care at all.

A car coming from the direction in which he was headed passed him and stopped. A man got out and came across the road. It was a man the gray personage did not want to see, a man he had been avoiding for months; he dropped the handle of the jack and stood erect for the encounter; he was not afraid, but his heart seemed to skip a beat and something in him said "Now!" with a tensing of every muscle. . . .

A buyer for Armour and Company remembered, when he saw the newspapers next morning, that he had noticed two cars parked on opposite sides of the road at the top of the hill. Two men were standing beside a black sedan. He had driven by, thinking nothing of it. "Gosh!" he said to himself, feeling suddenly a void at the pit of the stomach, "it must have been them! Two or three minutes later and I'd have seen it happen." He wondered uneasily whether he ought not to report to the sheriff what he had seen—but, after all, what had he to tell? The stock market reports were coming over his radio at the time and he hadn't noticed the license numbers. He could not even describe the men except that one was tall and dressed in gray. It would be bad business to get mixed up in anything like that—might mean appearances in court and loss of time from his job. So he said nothing.

The farmer in a battered flivver who passed a little later

saw only one man—engaged in taking out the jack from under a back wheel. The farmer, too, failed to notice the license numbers or to notice anything special about the man. Just a man with his back turned, stooped over.

There was, to be sure, an eyewitness to the grim little drama played out there beside the road under the fierce noonday glare in the short space of time between the passing of the buyer and of the farmer—but the beady little eyes of this witness were tuned to other than stupid human values. Human beings meant nothing to this redheaded citizen except as setters-up of the telephone poles that served so conveniently as his larder, and as the senseless takers-down of poles particularly well stocked with succulent grubs. He had been hatched right here beside the highway, and highway noise did not worry him at all. Just below him there on the ground a hot indignation was meeting a sudden, cold anger; but he hammered away unheeding, just under the crosstrees of his favorite pole, making the wood ring like an Indian war drum.

What happened next seemed unimportant to the feathered observer, though it was to affect, in one way or another, a great many different people, and would send the name of Keedora out all over the country—in screaming newspaper headlines, in police circulars, on voices over the radio. One minute the two men were talking—not loud, but in voices tense with conflict. Next minute a quick movement, an awkward, grotesque struggle—apparently for possession of a small object that glinted blue-black in the sunlight. The man in gray lost his Panama hat and it was trampled into the dust and weeds.

A shot.

The sound hardly disturbed the wide silence of the hot cornfields; a short, sharp crack like a slap or the snapping of a twig. But the gray man lay sprawled on the hard earth with his bare head in a patch of burdock and a red stain spreading slowly above his heart. He made two or three convulsive movements and lay still.

The woodpecker did not fly away, but he stopped his hammering for a moment and slid his body around to the back of the pole. A flock of crows got up from among the ranks of corn and flapped heavily away, cawing their protest. Nothing else was changed. The sun beat down into the putty-colored face of the dead man, the shrilling of the insects rose and fell in short waves of sound, and the bruised dock leaves gave out hot, thick smells.

The live man sat on the running board of the sedan and held his head in his hands. He felt surprised—the thing had happened so quickly, as though planned and rehearsed beforehand. Of course he had thought many times about killing the man who lay dead at his feet—during hot, sleepless nights and lonely hours on the road. But these thoughts had been dreams rather than definite, practical plans.

Now the thing was done, and could never be undone.

The man felt neither elated, nor remorseful, nor fearful of the consequences. Merely amazed, and a little sick. Blood always made him feel sick, though he had seen rivers of it. For a moment he was back in the Argonne.

He must decide what to do, though. He must think. It was hard to think. For some time he sat there in the sun, unable to bring his mind to a focus on the problem before him. A crowd of irrelevant memories clogged his consciousness. He saw himself as a freckled ten-year-old, fishing for catfish in the sluggish stream down there at the foot of the hill; he thought of a moonlit night in France, and of a letter a girl had once written him, and of his breakfast that morning. He noted calmly that a company of ants had found the dead man and were exploring his eyebrows and his upthrust chin.

A fast car whizzed by along the highway. The driver,

intent on the speedometer and the way ahead, saw nothing else. He was racing from Deland to Keedora on a bet and never knew how near he had come to front-page headlines and fame for a day. He won his bet, but missed the chance of a lifetime.

Out of the jumble in the killer's mind a plan slowly took shape. He drew a handkerchief from his pocket and carefully wiped the gun of all telltale marks. Holding it in the handkerchief he threw it from him into the tangle of weeds between the road and the fence. A small, bright something lay on the ground at his feet. He picked that up and tossed it away, too. The woodpecker from his perch on the telephone pole noted where it lodged in the fold of a thick, gray, hairy mullein leaf. He investigated it later, but found it to be nothing of importance. The man then opened the door of the black sedan and, picking up the limp, red-stained thing from the ground, thrust it inside and covered it with the lap robe. He went around to the back of the car and released the jack, put that inside, too, and locked the doors with care. He then crossed the road to his own parked car, got in and drove away.

Several automobiles passed, and more than one person noticed the black sedan deserted at the top of the hill. It seemed unimportant at the time, but afterward these people would get a great thrill out of remembering. "He must have been right there, inside!" they would say in awestruck tones. The nearest approach to drama that some of them would ever know.

One highway tramp in a rattletrap flivver actually stopped, and with a wary eye on the quiet landscape tried the locked doors of the sedan. He was not above picking up a tool kit or a blanket if it came handy. He looked through the glass and saw something in the bottom of the car under the lap robe. A sack of potatoes, he guessed. He thought of breaking the glass, but decided it was not worth the risk. He climbed back into his old wreck and clattered away.

The woodpecker saw all this. Later he saw a man come on foot through the cornfield. At a moment when no cars were in sight either way along the road the man climbed through the fence, unlocked the black sedan, got in and drove away.

These proceedings were far less interesting to the woodpecker than the faint gnawing of a grub inside the pole. Perhaps in the eye of Eternity the matters were of equal importance. The woodpecker made a few sharp taps with his mallet head, and the grub was his. He made it a part of himself and flew away through the sunshine.

CHAPTER 2

IN KEEDORA, where nothing would be known of the roadside tragedy for some hours, the hot afternoon wore by as usual. Sheriff Flagler, in shirtsleeves and without a collar, lay back in his old desk chair with his feet on his battered desk and slept. A bar of sunlight from a broken slat in the closed blind lay across his tanned cheek like a livid scar; an electric fan fluttered a lock of gray hair at his temple.

He was a big man, oldish, with a heavy walrus mustache that drooped lower on one side than the other and gave him an expression of gentle melancholy, but his eyes—when they happened to be open—were of an intense, keen blue that could be cold as ice. The fan hummed steadily, stirring up the stale air of the office with its odors of old tobacco, harsh soap, and old woodwork. A fly buzzed and bumbled against the drawn shade.

A watering-cart moved slowly up and down Main Street spreading its fan-shaped tail of spray that left the bricks dark and steaming almost as long as it took the cart to reach the next block.

Old Mr. Laubesheimer's handy boy, Willy, was making patterns on the sidewalk in front of the grocery store with the spray of a watering can, and the grocer himself was fussing with the ropes of his faded awning in the effort to bring its shade down a little lower over his wilting lettuces.

In the office of the Keedora Realty Company on the corner, above the drugstore, Miss Marsh was clacking away on her typewriter in spite of the heat. "In consideration of one dollar in hand paid and other valuable considerations—"

The street-car on its way to the cemetery turned the corner with a screech of wheels and Miss Marsh said

"Damn." She was alone in the office. Why couldn't they do something about that turn? Some dark night she would attend to it herself with a pot of grease and a wad of something on a stick. "All that certain parcel of land—"

Out along Fifth Street all the houses presented blank, shuttered faces to the sun.

In her room on the second floor of the old Slater house Milly Slater lay on her bed. She was a young thing, soft and pretty, naked under the light silk of her wrapper, and she had been crying.

The house belonged to the mansard and cupola period and had been built by Milly's grandfather. It was still called the Slater place, though Milly's father was dead and her mother remarried. There was a round bed of cannas and foliage plants in front of the house, but the true garden—a long, narrow strip shaded by trees and bright with flowers—lay behind.

Milly's room was on the garden side. She had not closed her blinds, for a big sugar maple cut off the glare, and through the window came now and then a wandering puff of fragrance from the mignonette border below.

Milly was not crying any more. At eighteen one cannot cry continuously for more than two hours or so even though one's heart is broken.

Harold was gone—he would not be back for two weeks. During their long-drawn-out farewells that morning she had tried to persuade him to give up this silly fishing trip and instead to take her to that vague country called "away." He just kept saying over and over, "But don't you see I can't? I promised the fellows and they're depending on me." If she had told him—but somehow she couldn't.

She hated herself, or thought she did. She hated her body that had betrayed her, and wished she could discard it as she had the rumpled dress that hung over the back of a chair.

What would her mother say when she found out?—as she must find out before long. She could imagine. Jim—her stepfather, gentle, ineffectual Jim Gordon—he would see her through. Jim was sweet. The thought of him was like a protecting arm around her. She turned toward the wall and slept.

Old Mrs. Paradise never slept in the afternoon, no matter how hot the weather. She sat on her high porch that was like a watchtower, rocking and tatting, and peering out between the vines to take note of all the small doings of the neighborhood.

Mrs. Paradise was, of course, the first person in Keedora—next to Grandma Breen and one other—to become aware that "something" had happened to Will Breen, president of the People's State Bank, ex-mayor, and prominent citizen.

It was late afternoon when Grandma Breen came out of the house next door to stand on the top step of the porch and look off down the street. The sunlight, beating almost horizontally from the west, fell flat against her bony figure in its faded cotton housedress. Her raised arm made a bar of shadow as thin as the shadow of a skeleton arm across her shrunken bosom; her work-gnarled hand made a cave of shadow for her eyes and threw her sharp chin and wrinkled, hollowed cheeks into strong relief.

"Will Breen's late getting home tonight," thought Mrs. Paradise, startled. The thing had never happened before during all the years. "The poor old soul is alone, too."

Harold Breen, she knew, had started off that morning for the camping trip he had been talking about for so long. The clatter of his ancient motor had waked Mrs. Paradise before sunup and she had gone to the window in her nightdress to watch him set out, the back of his flivver loaded with this and that under a stretched canvas.

"Maybe I'd better go over and talk to her," Mrs. Paradise

told herself. She rolled her tatting carefully and laid it on the little table at her elbow; she got to her feet and shook out her skirts, wrinkled from long sitting.

Presently she emerged from behind her vines and crossed the strip of lawn that separated the two houses.

"Will's kind of late tonight," said Mrs. Paradise, seating herself uninvited on the Breens' front steps.

"Yes—and I'm that worried!" Grandma Breen quavered in her high, old voice. "He said he'd be home by five and it's most six, now. He's never been a minute late for anything in all his life, I do believe. I've got a feeling something terrible's happened to him."

"Well," said Mrs. Paradise comfortingly, "it isn't as though he was a child. Will's past fifty, and he ought to be able to take care of himself by now. He went off right before lunch, didn't he?"

"Yes. He said he had to drive over to Deland to see a man on business. But he said he'd be back by five. I wish Harold was at home—he'd know what to do."

"If he's had an accident on the road you'd have heard about it before this," said Mrs. Paradise.

She felt a pleasant tingle of excitement, though of course she hoped nothing dreadful had happened.

A car turned the corner at the foot of the street, and the two old women watched its approach intently. But it wasn't William Breen's black sedan. It stopped in front of the Marshalls' house in the next block.

From across the street came the whine of the Johnsons' radio. They kept it on all the time; Mr. Johnson must have a terrible bill for electricity to pay every month. From off in the direction of the depot a train whistled.

"That's the six-eight," moaned Grandma Breen. "Oh, dear! I just know something awful's happened."

"Why don't you telephone over to Deland and find out what's keeping him," suggested Mrs. Paradise. "There's no use you pestering yourself this way. You look half sick—you'll be having one of your 'spells.' "

"Oh, I couldn't telephone. Anything like that would make Will wild. I wish Harold was home."

"Harold made an awful early start," said Mrs. Paradise. "I suppose Will let him go to get him away from that Slater girl for a while. I hear they want to get married and Will won't hear to it."

Her tone was a question rather than an assertion.

"Will's a hard man, sometimes," sighed Grandma Breen. "Milly Slater's a real sweet little thing, and I think young folks had ought to get married. It's natural."

Yes, Mrs. Paradise reflected, Will Breen was a hard man. And mighty "close," too. You'd think with all the money he was supposed to have he'd hire a maid instead of letting his old mother do all the work in that big house. Harold helped her a lot, of course—Mrs. Paradise had glimpsed him through the windows, making beds and washing dishes. But what kind of business was that for a young fellow? It would serve Will Breen right if—

Inside the house the telephone shrilled suddenly.

Mrs. Paradise jumped to her feet.

"You sit right here, Mrs. Breen, I'll answer it for you," she called over her shoulder as she ran across the porch to the open door.

"Deland calling Mr. William Breen," said the nasal voice of Jennie Wills, the telephone operator, into Mrs. Paradise's left ear.

"Mr. Breen isn't home right now." Her heart pounded.

"Well, hold the wire. Maybe my party will talk to you." A longish pause, and then: "Go ahead, Deland."

"Deland" spoke in a man's voice—courteous, but with an overtone of irritation. "This is Graves speaking, Mrs. Breen."

Mrs. Paradise saw no reason to give her name.

"Yes?"

"Mr. Breen was to have met me here in Deland early this afternoon—on that Cushman business. I've been waiting around all day, but he hasn't showed up. I suppose he was detained. Now I've got to make the six-thirty-five out. When Mr. Breen comes home, please tell him I'll get in touch with him again when I come through this way next week."

"You mean—?" gasped Mrs. Paradise, poised on tiptoe to reach the mouthpiece that was set too high for her inches. "Mr. Breen never got to Deland? Why—!" But the line was dead; the "party" had hung up.

Mrs. Paradise stood in the half-dark hallway that smelled of floor polish and old wallpaper, and faintly of the supper Will Breen would not be needing, still clutching the telephone.

She tingled with excitement to the tips of her toes—inside the "Comfy-Last" shoes that cost her two dollars and seventeen cents a pair at Thistlewaite's sale a year ago. "Something" had certainly happened to Will Breen. Had he been kidnaped like that banker who was carried off from his own house in Eldora and tortured so that he would never be the same again ? Had he been—murdered?

"Number, please," said the telephone against her chest.

"I want to talk to Sheriff Flagler, Jennie," said Mrs. Paradise into the telephone. "He won't be at his office; try Mrs. Stark's boardinghouse."

When a tired voice answered, she said, "The sheriff, please, Mrs. Stark."

"Call later, can't you ? He's eating."

"I've got to talk to him right away. Something terrible's happened. Will Breen's disappeared."

In this way the first news of the tragedy went out into the stagnant evening. Jennie Wills was destined to have a busy time at her switchboard for the next few hours.

CHAPTER 3

OLD MRS. PARADISE ran back through the hall to the porch, the bad news hot on her lips. All the nerves in her dried-up little body sang with excitement. She had not been so vividly alive for years. Not, to be exact, since the night three years ago when Tom Bronson came home drunk and started to kill his wife with the stove-poker.

Grandma Breen lay, limp as a dishrag, in one of the porch chairs.

"Oh! what is it?" she moaned. "I just know something terrible's happened."

"I hate to tell you," said Mrs. Paradise. "But I guess you've got to know. Will never got to Deland. The man he was to meet over there just called up."

Grandma Breen said nothing at all. Her mouth opened and shut two or three times and then she slowly toppled sideways. She hung for a moment over the arm of the chair and then slid to the floor of the porch and lay still. One of her "spells."

Mrs. Paradise was unable to cope with the situation alone. She ran across the street to the Johnsons'. She hadn't spoken to either Tom Johnson or Jessie for over a year—not since what happened at the church strawberry festival—but all that was forgotten now.

Tina Johnson and that Price boy were sitting very close together in the porch hammock. They started apart at Mrs. Paradise's explosive arrival.

"Help!" cried Mrs. Paradise. "It's Grandma Breen— one of her heart attacks. She's had a shock."

She turned and ran back across the street with the girl and boy at her heels. Tom Johnson, hearing the disturbance, came to the door. He called back into the house to

Jessie and then hurried across the street, too.

Between them the two men carried the little old woman's inert body upstairs to the back bedroom, while Jessie—told by Tina what had happened—went to the telephone and called Dr. Parsons.

"Where's everybody?" asked Tom Johnson in his amiable rumble. "Will? Harold? Nobody 'round?"

The story of Harold's trip and Will's disappearance came tumbling from Mrs. Paradise, all in a breath.

When the doctor came, it all had to be told again. They stood about the big, old-fashioned bed in the heavy heat of the bedroom, waiting for the doctor's verdict.

"She's coming out of it," he said at last. "Some day she won't. But we've got to have a nurse—somebody call the hospital and tell them to send Miss Chester over."

Wally Price was nearest the door. "I'll go," he volunteered.

A few minutes later he came galloping back upstairs to say that Sheriff Flagler had arrived, and wanted to talk to somebody. The "somebody" indicated was, of course, Mrs. Paradise. Wally Price and the Johnson girl were at her heels, but she hardly noticed them.

The sheriff had stopped at home long enough after the telephone message to finish his supper. A man's got to eat, and in his experience things were never as urgent as people on the telephone thought they were.

"What's all this about Will Breen's having disappeared?" he wanted to know.

Mrs. Paradise told what little there was to tell, spinning out the story with much unnecessary detail.

"Looks queer, all right," he admitted—"Will Breen being the kind he is. Like clockwork. But lots of things look damn queer for a while and turn out to be nothing to make a fuss about. You tell Grandma Breen to take it easy. I'll inquire 'round, and maybe take a run over to Deland.

Where's Harold?"

He was told about Harold's fishing trip and his departure in the early morning.

"Hm. Know where he's gone to? Might want to get hold of him."

"Some lake up in Wisconsin," Mrs. Paradise thought. "Probably Mrs. Breen knows, but we can't ask her right now."

"Well, there's no hurry. I'll just help myself to the telephone."

He called his colleague, Sheriff Witherspoon, of the next county, at Deland.

"Witherspoon? Flagler talking. Say, you know Will Breen? Yes, the banker. Seems he started for Deland along about noon today to meet a party over there by the name of Graves. Yes, that's right. Well, he never showed up, Graves says, and he didn't get back here. Have a look around. Take a run out the road, will you? I'll meet you. Sure. Thanks."

He turned from the telephone, went heavily down the steps to his car and chugged away.

Wally Price was leaving, too.

"Where are you going, Wally?" the Johnson girl asked in a low voice.

"Out to see what's doing. Why, girl, this is *news!* Maybe it's our break. Front-page stuff, and nobody knows about it yet but us!" He made no pretence of hiding his bubbling enthusiasm. "Might be a chance in it for a job on a city paper and a "Mrs. Price" on your calling cards—if any. At least it ought to run to a nice bit of change."

"I think you're—horrid," said the girl. "You act as though you were tickled to death."

"That's the newspaper game," said Wally.

He took himself seriously as a member of the fourth estate, being fresh from a college course in journalism and the editorship of a college paper. The fact that the Keedora

Bugle, though urged, had felt no need of his services was a fact that rankled.

"Of course," he said, "it's too bad if the old geezer's been killed or anything—but if you think I'm not tickled at the break for us, you're crazy."

He turned again to go.

"Where are you going?" the girl insisted. "I'm going with you."

"Well, come along, then. I can't stand here arguing. I've got business."

The two youngsters slipped away into the evening, and presently Mrs. Paradise heard the shocking clatter of Wally Price's battered old car.

CHAPTER 4

MILLY SLATER didn't want any supper, but if she didn't go downstairs her mother would come up and make a fuss. She dabbed her eyes with boric acid till some of the redness disappeared. Powder helped. Mother wouldn't notice anything—she was always too busy at supper being angry with Jim to pay much attention to anything else. Jim would notice, of course, but he wouldn't say anything.

Poor Jim! No amount of scolding would make a businessman of him. Why had he and her mother married? It was one of the mysteries.

Milly slipped into her place at the table between her self-absorbed mother and the gentle, kindly creature that was her stepfather. She bowed her head while Mrs. Gordon, who made a point of it, recited the stereotyped "We thank Thee, O Lord—" of an old-fashioned "grace." There was little enough of grace in her manner of doing it.

Raising her eyes after the pious "Amen," Milly encountered the commiserating eyes of her stepfather. His look seemed to reach out and touch her like a caress. He saw through the powder to the puffy redness of tear-drenched eyes. She had expected that. But for the first time she realized that he knew the shameful, terrible thing she had not had enough courage to tell Harold that morning during their long talk under the lilacs. Probably he had known as long as she herself. Somehow, she was glad he knew. The comfort of his affection, his understanding, enfolded her. A little of her fear left her.

"I suppose it is too much to hope that you collected the interest on that note today." Mrs. Gordon addressed her husband in a tone dripping with contempt.

"I hardly expected to. The poor fellow hasn't any

money, as I told you," he answered gently. It was a nightly ritual.

"I'll wager you never even went out there to see him about it," Mrs. Gordon snorted.

Jim Gordon said nothing, and kept his eyes on his plate. A slow red mounted to his prominent cheekbones. He was a sensitive creature and in all the years had never been able to build up an adequate negative adaptation to this sort of thing. Probably he never would.

"Of course my opinions and wishes are of no importance," Mrs. Gordon rasped on. "All I have to do with the business is merely to own it, and put up money for the losses."

Her husband was goaded to a reply. "There haven't been any losses yet—really—"

"Well, if there haven't, it's no fault of yours, Jim Gordon," she taunted him.

"You are probably correct," he said, without rancor. "I am sure you could manage the business much better yourself than I have been able to do. As you may recall, when you first insisted that I undertake the management of the business for you, I told you I feared I was not cut out for a real estate man."

"Manage it myself!" she cried, exasperated. "What a laugh the town would get out of that! And while I was managing the business, what would you be doing? Just what *do* you think you were cut out for?"

"God knows!" he sighed wearily.

"Don't be sacrilegious," she reproved him.

Silence ensued. The evening ritual had been completed. For the next twenty mouthfuls, at least, no word would be spoken.

But to Milly the blessed silence seemed fragile, like a thin film of brittle glass that the tiniest sound would fracture. She laid her knife down on the edge of her plate with infinite care to make no noise, and was afraid to eat because it seemed to her that the working of her jaws would resound in the stillness.

Through the open window a faint puff of hot air, heavy with the sweetness of the dark garden outside under the stars, slipped between the limp curtains to mingle with the coffee fragrance and food odors of the supper table. Somewhere down the street someone was strumming lazily on a ukelele.

Supper was over at last and Milly escaped into the garden—to her favorite refuge under a huge old snowball bush whose branches arching over nearly to the ground made a doughnut-shaped tent of green around its thick clump of stems. Here when she was very tiny she had used to set out feasts of buttercups and violets for the fairies.

She lay in the warm grass and looked up through the pattern of leaves to the moon and the soft stars. The night enfolded her—understanding, gentle, concealing, like Jim Gordon's love for her. Some people believed those stars, thousands of light-years away, affected the little lives of people on earth. Silly. Perhaps not. Life is all of a piece. We don't live it—it lives us.

She thought of Harold, chugging along northward on unfamiliar roads under this same moon. He and "the fellows" would be talking, cracking silly jokes, perhaps singing. Harold loved to sing while he drove. She felt a little guilty over having kept him so long that morning, when he intended to make an early start. Almost noon when she finally let him go. The bitter mood of her afternoon had passed. When he came back, perhaps his Uncle Will—

She need not have worried about what Harold's Uncle Will would do or not do. By that time Will Breen had been dead for hours.

Something was happening back at the house. She heard voices. Someone rolled back the door of the garage, and she heard the stutter of a starting engine. She scrambled out of her retreat.

The car was in the driveway. The lights shone straight ahead against the gate, making its white bars stand out like bars of fire against the darkness. Somebody was opening the gate. She saw it was young Tom Granger. Her mother was in the front seat of the car, next to Jim, at the wheel. A man was climbing into the back seat. As she drew close, she saw it was Big Tom Granger, father of young Tom. What was it he had in his hand ? A—rifle!

"Hate to bother you folks this way," Big Tom rumbled in his deep voice, "but my car's all to bits. Young Tom here's got it strewed all over the garage. And seeing as how I'm a deputy—"

Milly opened the door of the car on her side and climbed in, over the hard stock of another rifle.

Young Tom came up at the moment.

"That you, Milly? Say, you better stay home."

But Milly did not move. She did not know what was happening, but she was afraid. Not for worlds would she have stayed behind alone in the empty house.

"Get on in, son," growled the elder Granger. "We ain't got time to argue. We got one woman along anyhow—might's well have two." He leaned over the front seat. "Say, Gordon, you got a gun on you?"

"No," Jim Gordon's quiet voice answered. "I won't need a gun."

"Maybe you'd better have it, Jim," said Mrs. Gordon fussily. "Milly can run upstairsand get it for you out of the drawer—"

Jim made no answer except to set the car in motion.

"Where are we going? What's happened?" Milly asked in a whisper of the boy beside her.

The rifle she had stumbled over was his. He was holding it now between his knees, and she could feel against her the hard lump of the revolver at his belt. She trembled a little.

"You don't know?" he said, surprised. "Where you been?"

"Oh, down in the garden," she answered vaguely.

"It's Mr. Breen," the boy explained eagerly. "He started for Deland some time this morning, but he never got there. Something's happened to him. Maybe"—there was awe and excitement in his voice—"he's been murdered. The sheriff's out now, looking for him along the road to Deland. Dad's a deputy, and he brought me along. I'm a dead shot, you know."

Mr. Breen! Harold's uncle! The surge of emotion that swept through Milly was so intense that it frightened her. She could hardly breathe and her heart pounded. Disappeared. Dead, perhaps. It was wicked to feel glad—but how could she help it? She clenched her hands till the nails bit into her palms, but no sound came from her.

"Of course maybe he's been kidnaped," Young Tom went on. "Somebody's watching the house for a phone call or a ransom note or something. But that ain't likely to do any good. They could have him across the state line by now, like the way they done with that banker over in Eldora last year. They took him all the way to North Dakota, and they tortured the poor guy something terrible. Burned his feet pretty near off, and—"

"Don't!" said Milly in a strangled voice.

"Lay off, son," growled the elder Granger "You're getting the girl all scared up."

By this time they had left the town behind. Milly saw the big white gate of the cemetery come up ahead in the light of the car and go sliding by into darkness again. They were rolling along between the cornfields. There were fireflies in the weeds along the roadway, and many lights that were not fireflies.

Their car was one in a long procession that streamed

along the road like a string of stars. Other cars were coming up behind them. Amazing how quickly the whole community had been set in motion. It was not late—barely nine o'clock.

They dipped over the edge of the bluff for the long descent to the river and the bridge. Little points of light could be seen up and down the river.

"Flashlights," said the Granger boy. "Looking for him."

"They won't find no corpse in the river," opined the elder Granger. "Ain't hardly enough water to wet anybody above the ankles."

But when they got down to the river, he touched Jim on the shoulder and asked him to stop.

Many cars were parked there on each side of the approach to the bridge, standing at odd angles over the shoulders of the road.

The two Grangers got out, but Milly sat where she was, and the two in the front seat also stayed in the car. Jim killed the engine and switched off the lights and suddenly it was very still and blue, there in the moonlight. The moon lay in moving, shifting flakes on the surface of the sluggish stream, and picked out the bright metalwork of the cars, and the crisscross pattern of the bridge.

Only last night Milly and Harold had sat here in Harold's old car, clasped in each other's arms. The same fragrance of the rank sweet clover, the same shrilling of insects, the same mournful night bird crying the same hoarse lament in the darkness—

People in a shadowy group were clustered along the rail of the bridge. Someone dropped a stone that fell into the water with a loud "gloop," and a woman's voice said sharply, "Stop that this minute, Pete! Don't you know enough not to be throwing stones at a time like this?"

Mr. Granger's deep bass boomed up and down the stream at the twinkling flashlights and the scattered splashings, "Hey, fellows, found anything yet?"

A confused shouting answered him. Before long he and the boy came back and climbed into the car.

"May's well drive along, Jim," said the elder Granger.

They drove across the bridge that rattled hollowly under the wheels of the car, past the watchers at the rail, and down among the fields again.

"How much farther do you want to go, Granger?" Jim Gordon asked over his shoulder.

"Oh, a piece farther—till we meet up with the sheriff. He called Witherspoon on the telephone and they'll come together somewhere along here."

Jim Gordon drove steadily along, saying nothing.

The whole countryside was awake. Farmhouses blazed with lights, though it was past farm bedtime. A group of people standing beside a rural delivery mailbox called out to them as they passed, but they did not stop.

At Bridger—a crossroads store and a gas pump—a number of cars were parked and many people were standing about in groups. An old woman in a sunbonnet with her hands clasped across her stomach under an ample kitchen apron; a tired-looking girl with damp straggles of hair across her forehead and a heavy baby in her arms; a giggling carload of high-school youngsters from Deland; men in boots and overalls, carrying rifles; a man in a Palm Beach suit, with a Panama hat on the back of his head—running about telling everybody, "Now keep calm. Don't get excited."

Jim parked, and behind him other cars kept swooping in and stopping. Like a flock of vultures, Milly thought. The crowd was swelling minute by minute. The scene was queer and dramatic—there in the heart of the thick, hot night, lighted in fierce, stabbing streaks by the level lights of automobiles, with the serene moon sailing overhead.

The two Grangers got out of the car.

"Guess Flagler and Witherspoon must a' met here," said the elder Granger. "We'll be back pretty quick."

He went off, trailed by his lanky son—both carrying rifles—to join the main knot of men milling around the steps of the store.

"I'm going over there, too," said Mrs. Gordon after a time. She got down heavily. "Come along, Jim."

CHAPTER 5

MILLY SLATER huddled into a corner of the car's back seat. She felt sick with the excitement and the war of emotions in her heart. The sight of so many people milling about in the darkness of the crossroads brought home to her the horror of what had happened—gave the thing for her three dimensions and a hideous reality. She cried a little and made herself as small as possible in her corner.

Presently she saw someone coming slowly along the rank of parked cars as though looking for somebody. In the beam of a headlight his face suddenly stood out sharp and startling against the night. It was Sheriff Flagler.

He paused beside the car in which she sat and said in that slow, kindly voice of his, "That you, Milly Slater, all hunched up in the dark?" He opened the door of the car and got in beside her. "I'm going to sit here with you a few minutes, Milly. There's two or three things I want to ask you."

"I don't know anything, Mr. Flagler," she answered in a low voice between her trembling lips. "How could I know anything?"

"Thought maybe you might know where we could reach Harold," he said. "Mind if I smoke?" He took a pipe out of his pocket, filled it deliberately, and struck a match. "Some lake up in Wisconsin, they tell me."

"It's called 'Pine Cone Lake,' " Milly said. She was not shaking so terribly now. There was something reassuring in the bulk and gentleness of the big man beside her in the dark.

"I don't know just where it is. There isn't any post office. Harold said not to try to write."

"He won't hardly have got there by this time," the

sheriff mused. "Have you any idea what route he meant to take?"

"No," Milly answered. "I just know he meant to stop in Des Moines to pick up one of the boys who were going along—but he wouldn't be in Des Moines now, and I don't know the name of the boy, anyway."

"Know if he's got a radio along?"

"Harold didn't have one," said the girl, "but there was another car going—one of the others might have a radio."

"Well, it looks like we can't get word to him. But maybe he'll see the bad news in a newspaper along the way somewhere. His grandma wants him home, I expect." He talked in a quiet, conversational way, as though nothing very grave were the question. "You and Harold's kind of sweethearts, I hear."

"We've been engaged a year."

"Fixing to get married soon?"

Milly did not answer. She was beginning to feel afraid. What was the sheriff asking her these questions for?

"I been told," the sheriff went on, "that you'd have been married before this except that Will Breen kind of stood in the way. What'd he have to do with it? Harold's over twenty-one, isn't he?"

Milly hesitated. She didn't want to talk about Harold and herself; but after all she could not very well refuse to answer.

"Harold's an orphan, you know. His Uncle Will is his guardian. There's some money coming to Harold, but, according to his father's will, Mr. Breen is to hold it 'at his discretion' till Harold is twenty-five."

"Hard feelings in that, I wouldn't wonder," said the sheriff. "Harold's working, isn't he?"

"Yes. But we can't get married on what they pay him at the bank. Mr. Breen isn't fair to Harold, Mr. Flagler."

"Will Breen's a hard man, Milly. And he just can't bear to let go of a dollar that comes his way—whether it's his or somebody else's. Did he and Harold have any quarrel that you know about?"

"What do you mean?" cried Milly, in a sudden panic. "You don't mean you suspect Harold of—" She choked.

"I hope to God, Milly," said the sheriff fervently, "that Harold hasn't done anything—stupid. Harold's a fine young fellow. I like him. Known him, too, since he was a little shaver. But there it is, girl. If something's happened to Will Breen, Harold could have done it, and we both know it. He had reason enough."

Milly wanted to cry out. Her mouth opened, but no sound issued. She lay against the cushions of the car, half paralyzed with fright and horror.

"What I came over to ask you, Milly," the sheriff said gravely, "is what time Harold left you this morning."

Milly did not answer.

"You can't help Harold by not answering, nor by lying to me, girl," he said.

"He came to say good-bye," Milly said, in a strangled voice. "It was very early. He waked me up."

"How?"

"He stood in the garden and called to me. The other bedroom windows are on the other side of the house. Nobody heard him but me. I went down in the garden and talked to him. I didn't want to let him go. I wanted him to take me away—anywhere."

"How long were you there in the garden?"

"Not very long. We were afraid somebody would come. We drove out to Catamount Spring. We go there sometimes when we—want to be by ourselves."

"What time would that be?"

"I don't know exactly, but it was ten o'clock when Harold looked at his watch. He was surprised to see how late it was. You see he'd meant to get an early start and was supposed to be almost to Des Moines by that time."

"Anybody see you out there?"

"Nobody."

"Harold drove you home then?"

"No. He was in such a hurry that I told him to let me off at the cemetery. I came home on the streetcar."

"Takes about thirty-five minutes to drive in from Catamount," said the sheriff. "Harold must have got out of town, then, about ten-thirty-five to ten-forty."

"Yes," said the girl, "and—Mr. Breen didn't leave till half-past eleven. I'm sure I heard someone say that. And—"

"That's right," agreed the sheriff. "Now you just take it easy, and everything will be all right for you and Harold. —I hope," he added to himself.

There was, unfortunately, something like stopping on the road, and of course the time must be checked. Bud Carson, who had the gas station near the cemetery, might know something. He patted the girl kindly on the shoulder.

"I'm going to leave you in peace now," he said. "Don't worry any more than you can help, and when Harold gets back, tell him I want to see him, the first thing."

He climbed out of the car and went away, across to the store. People kept stopping him. Milly supposed it was to ask him questions. She noticed that the store—a long, narrow, wooden structure with a silly false front—was lighted from end to end. Someone had called the storekeeper from his beauty sleep, and, dressed in trousers, suspenders, and a pajama top, he was doing a land-office business in gas and pop and candy.

The crowd had increased. People from Keedora meeting friends and acquaintances from Deland were "visiting"—sitting together on the running boards of parked automobiles. A tired child was complaining in a tearful whine, and asking over and over, "Why'n't we go home now?"

Milly, in her dark corner, cried a little—with relief after

the dreadful moment of fear. Of course Harold couldn't have—How could she have thought for a minute that perhaps—

Her stepfather was standing at the door of the car.

"You all right, Milly?" he asked anxiously. The moonlight lay blue on the planes of his forehead, on the jut of his cheekbones. He laid a hand gently over hers. "Don't be frightened."

His voice was very tender and somehow it made her tears flow more freely.

"It's pretty awful, Jim."

"Your mother and our passengers ought to be able to tear themselves away pretty soon," said Jim. "It's hard on you. You should not have come."

He got into the car—into the front seat behind the wheel. Huddled in her corner, Milly wept.

A youngster, running in and out among the cars, put his hand in through the open door of the car beside them and sounded the horn. Its hoarse bleat seemed to have the effect of breaking up the meeting, for presently the main group of people around the store began to dissolve and straggle away. Engines began to whir. The two Grangers and their rifles turned up, and at last Mrs. Gordon appeared.

"We might as well go home, Jim," she said, with disappointment in her voice. "Nobody knows anything, or even seems likely to know anything."

Jim said nothing. He started the engine, wheeled— spraying light from the headlamps in a wide circle.

And presently they were on the road again, with the moon, the night perfumes, and the shrilling of insects. One in a long line of dark cars, each carrying its load of honest citizens home to bed, after the most exciting evening of years.

CHAPTER 6

IN ONE OF THE CARS rode Wally Price and his Tina. Wally was jubilant.

"What a break!" he gloated. "What a break! And, oh, boy! what I'm going to do with it. Maybe it will run to a job, woman. A job in the city. If it does, will you hop off with me, Tina? Of course you will; you needn't bother to answer."

Wally was an expert one-handed driver, but the ecstatic hug he gave her made the car swerve sharply.

"That wasn't so good," objected Tina mildly. She was a placid girl.

"Put your faith in Poppa, and hold on tight. I mean hold on tight to Poppa, woman. Gee! I'm so happy I could sing."

"It's not right to talk that way about poor Mr. Breen," Tina reproved him.

"I'm not talking about 'poor Mr. Breen'—I'm talking about us, if you get what I mean. U S—us."

"Just the same it's horrible, and you oughtn't to say you're happy about it."

"Of course it's horrible. The more horrible the better from the newspaper angle. Just think, it may have happened right here where we are this minute."

"What do you think happened, Wally?"

"Well, of course nobody knows. You heard them talking back there. Witherspoon's all for kidnaping. Flagler doesn't say much, but you can see he thinks it's murder."

"Who could have done a thing like that?"

"Why, I guess there must be a hundred people around here who could have done it. Who did do it? That's different. If you ask me, it's somebody right in Keedora. Might be somebody in the crowd back there—perhaps the person in the car up ahead."

"Oh, no," said the girl decidedly. "That's our washer-woman's car. Mrs. Triplett wouldn't murder anybody."

Wally whooped. Tina did not quite know why Wally laughed so much at the things she said, but she did not mind. He had a funny, high laugh that ended with a sort of gulp. She liked to hear it—it made her feel sort of comfortable inside.

"Mrs. Triplett has false teeth," Tina elaborated. "They click when she talks. She lives over on Bank Street. We have to watch her or she puts in too much blueing."

"Well," said Wally, "we'll count Mrs. Triplett out if you say so. How about the car ahead of hers? Maybe the murderer is in that one."

"Perhaps," said Tina doubtfully. "But I think it's the Smith's car."

"Who's behind us? Do you know that?"

"Why, of course. It's the Stevenses. They've got the baby along."

"Tina," said Wally solemnly, "you're a wonder. I can see where you'll be a great help to an ambitious reporter. You observe. I'll bet, though, you can't tell the color of Sheriff Witherspoon's tie."

She thought for a minute.

"Gray and blue," she said triumphantly.

"And it had a thread of green running through it. He had on a gray suit, and a silver belt buckle with his initials on it, and a handkerchief with a blue hem in his pocket, and—"

"That's enough! That's enough!"

"He's sort of cute, I think," said Tina complacently.

"Sheriff Flagler isn't 'cute,' " suggested Wally.

"Poor man! You can see he has no woman to look after him. There was a button off his vest, and that blackish string he uses for a necktie was tied all crooked."

"This is getting interesting," said Wally—not laughing

any more. "Who did you see that looked queer?"

"Like a murderer, you mean?" Tina was enjoying her success. "Of course there were some people I didn't know—There was a man standing by a tree. He looked sort of sick; his face was kind of putty-colored. But he was smiling like anything, and his eyes! He sort of gave me the shivers."

"By Heaven, the villain!" said Wally dramatically. "A lead at last! Where would you suggest looking for him?"

"I think he works in Hathaway's garage," said Tina.

Wally whooped again, and Tina laughed with him.

"Do you hear things, too, Tina?" Wally asked when he had got his breath.

"I heard Bud Carson—who has the gas station near the cemetery—tell Sheriff Flagler that Harold Breen stopped there for gas a few minutes before twelve."

Wally was serious in a moment.

"That," he said, "is damned important. I must find Bud right away."

"He passed us just a few minutes ago," said Tina.

Wally stepped on the throttle and slid by the Triplett car and the car ahead.

"It *is* the Smiths," said Tina. "I thought it was. And they have Buster along. He's asleep."

The Smiths were talking about William Breen, like everyone else in the long procession.

"Yes, it will make a difference," Mr. Smith was saying. "The other directors may be willing to renew the note, now. They wouldn't have forced me except for Will Breen."

"Then—you'll be able to keep your business? We won't have to go away? Oh! I'm glad!"

"We won't be the only ones to feel glad," said Mr. Smith. "I don't believe there's anyone in Keedora who will be really sorry to know that Will Breen is gone and won't ever come back. Not even Grandma Breen."

"That's—horrible," said the woman. "After all, he was

her son. I can't believe I'd ever—if it was Buster—" She hugged closer the sleeping child in her arms.

"Oh, it will be a shock to the old lady, but he treated her pretty mean. She ought to be left comfortable for the rest of her life."

"It's Harold she loves, of course."

"If they pin the thing on Harold, that will be hard on Grandma Breen, all right. And it looks kind of bad for Harold."

"To think of a thing like this happening right here in Keedora!" Mrs. Smith wept a few easy tears into the woolly shawl that enfolded her son. The night air flowed by, almost cool with the motion of the car. A car up ahead honked hoarsely.

And in more than one farmhouse among the cornfields, where lights still burned on this night of excitement, a husband and wife were telling each other that—though it seemed sort of horrible to say it—if Will Breen really was dead perhaps something could be done, after all, about the mortgage.

The murderer? How was he feeling? He was aware of neither triumph nor remorse—merely a sort of surprise, such as a paper knife might feel at finding itself thrust into the heart of a man. He had been no more than the weapon in the hand of something far stronger than himself. He felt very weary, and as drained of emotion as an empty suit of clothes hanging in a closet. The moment he laid himself on his bed he went to sleep.

CHAPTER 7

A NIGHT OF BREATHLESS HEAT lay over Keedora and its enfolding cornfields. One of those nights that the corn loves with every cell of its rank growth, from its shallow roots to its plumed crest twelve feet and more above the fat earth. People lie and swelter through such a night, and even the strongest-hearted feel the oppression of unnamed fears, and awake unrefreshed and drained of energy to face the white-hot day.

But the corn ripens.

Milly Slater awoke in the first gray of dawn—that most mournful moment of the twenty-four-hour cycle, when life is at its lowest ebb. The window was a vague rectangle of gray; the dresser, clothed in the silly flounces she had made for it in a time of happiness, stood—a forlorn little ghost—holding in its arms the shadowy dark shield of the mirror.

Milly wished she had not had to awake—that her body was lying there on the bed growing cold in the morning light. But people cannot die easily like that, just by wishing. She was young; she would probably have to go on living for a long time. She saw the long years ahead of her in intolerable perspective. Why do people have to live? she thought. Nobody is happy.

Love! Why do poets sing of love as something beautiful? Love is terrible—too strong, too shattering. Youth is not a time of joy as the old seem to recall it, but a time of cruel and bitter strife.

The birds were beginning their sunrise concert of twitterings and whistlings in the trees of the garden. The gray of the window began to show the tracery of branches and a faint flush of rose, like a delicate old Japanese print. The beauty of it made the desolation of her heart more poignant. Milly closed her eyes against the new day, and two scalding tears oozed out between the lids to fall with a damp plop on the hot pillow.

The thought of Jim Gordon's revolver brought her an odd sense of comfort. There was, after all, always a way of escape. With her eyes shut, she could see it as clearly as though it were actually before her. She had come on it once when putting Jim's freshly laundered collars away in the top drawer of his chiffonier, lying cold and blue and hard under a neat pile of handkerchiefs.

Was that a step in the garden? Milly held her breath and her heart seemed to stop. Something soft and light struck the screen with a gentle thud. She knew what it was—a rose, broken from the bush below the window. It was not the first time—

Milly slipped from between the hot sheets and went silently on bare feet to the window. A shadowy shape among the rosebushes and a pale, upturned face. She raised the screen and leaned out.

Harold was there. He called to her softly to come down. She put a finger to her lips and retreated back into the room. Slippers; a dark robe. She was opening her door inch by careful inch; she was in the dark well of the stair with a hand on the rail to steady her light steps; she was sliding back the bolt of the door. . . .

It was still dark on the porch, behind the screening vines—dark and warm and sweet with the scent of flowers and dewy grass. The birds were making a great clamor, and a greenish light was climbing up the sky. Arms! They were about her, holding her close against a strong, young body. A heart, not her own, beat against her heart; warm lips touched her forehead, her eyes, her hair, and settled clingingly against her lips. Love was alive again.

"Milly!"

"Harold!" His cheeks were wet. Holding each other

close, they moved down the garden path, away from the house, to their bench behind the lilacs.

"I came back," he said. "It all seemed so futile going away without you. You were right. We should have gone away together. We'll go now. A long way off—out to Montana or somewhere. Uncle Will can go to hell; we'll make out, somehow."

Harold didn't know! Then—he couldn't have—In the fierce joy of her relief she laughed and cried like a little idiot. Not till then did she realize that in her heart had been a fear she had not dared to name to herself.

"Say you'll come, Milly. Now."

He hadn't done it, but people suspected him. The sheriff suspected him. If she told him, he would stay, and perhaps they would put him behind bars, and bring him to trial. And she wanted to get away, with her lover, into a new world and a bright new day. Everything would be all right if they could get away.

"Milly! What's the matter, Milly? You look so queer."

"It's all right, Harold," she said, her mind made up. "Wait here for me. I'll be right back."

She was quick and careful, but somebody heard. Somebody had been lying awake like her in the hot dawn, had heard the car drive up and stop at the back of the garden, had heard Milly's light step along the hall. Heard her come back.

On the way out once more with her bag in her hand, Milly was startled and almost cried out at the apparition of a tall figure in the lower hall, by the door. Her stepfather.

"You're going away, Milly."

It was not a question. In the dimness of the shadowy hall his eyes burned strangely.

"Yes. Please don't try to stop me."

"You haven't told him?"

"No."

For a long minute he said nothing, standing there over her, holding her with a hand on her shoulder. "The best way, perhaps—for everybody," he said at last. "Milly, you know I love you. That I would do anything to help you."

"I know." She held her face up to his kiss.

"Don't write," he said. "Don't write to anybody till all this is over. Have you any money?"

"A little. I suppose Harold has some. It doesn't matter. We'll manage—somehow."

"Wait."

She watched him go into the room at the end of the hall—known as the "study." A little safe stood there in a corner. Her mother kept the housekeeping money in it, and sometimes when there had been late collections, after the bank closed, Jim brought home money from the office to keep overnight. He was not gone long. When he came back he pressed into her hand a roll of bills.

She looked from the money in her hand to the grave face above her.

"But—Mother—"

He closed her fingers around the bills.

"Don't worry," he said. "It's little enough. Your mother owes you more than that, my poor child."

From the door she looked back and saw him still standing there by the stair. A lump came in her throat. He did love her. Probably, she thought, in a flash of insight, he loved her far more than Harold did. He made a motion to her to go. . . .

CHAPTER 8

GRANDMA BREEN saw the sun rise, too, on that day of search and questioning and conjecture. She lay, incredibly frail and waxy, in the big black walnut bed with the little insets of blue tile that had been part of her marriage gear.

Almost fifty-two years now. She had been eighteen. Her father built the house as a wedding present. It was a small house for those times, but a big house now—with absurdly high ceilings, a front and back parlor and a "den."

What was that odd sound? Grandma Breen turned her head a little on the pillow. Oh, yes, the nurse, sleeping—a little too loudly—on a cot by the dresser.

The room was very crowded. The big bed took up all the space. That time when Will was planning to marry, he had moved her and the big bed into this little back bedroom. The marriage plans failed and Will remained a bachelor, but Grandma Breen had never got back the front bedroom. For years the thing had lain in her heart, a focus of bitterness and resentment. There was, she realized, now no reason why she should not move back. It should be done tomorrow. Today it was nice just to lie here and listen to the nurse snore.

And there was the cast-iron figure of a little black boy in a red shirt and blue pants, very realistically painted, that used to stand at the curb holding out an iron ring for horses that no longer required hitching. Will had the iron boy taken up—remarkable how deep the post he stood on was planted in the ground—and would have had him destroyed. But Grandma Breen rescued him and had him stored away in the attic, with the old Saratoga trunk that had been new to hold the finery for her wedding trip to Niagara.

The iron boy should go back to his place where she could see him from her front window. It gave her a pleasant feeling to think of having him there again, holding out his black hand clasping the iron ring. Harold would not mind. Harold was a good boy. He could marry that pretty little Slater girl now and they would live with her in the old house.

Grandma Breen was glad she had not died last night. It would be agreeable to live a little longer and see these things done.

What an uproar the birds were making over the coming of another day! They acted as excited as though the sun came up only once in a lifetime instead of once every twenty-four hours.

She wished the nurse would wake up. And then she realized with a sudden thrill of pleasure that there was no reason why she should not wake the nurse. Her nurse; there to wait on her. A little bell stood on a stand by the bed; she had just strength enough to reach it and shake it a little.

The nurse came awake all of a piece. A moment ago she was lying there sleeping her head off, and here she was standing by the bed feeling Grandma's pulse.

"I think," said Grandma," I should like a cup of tea and a slice of milk toast. I've just remembered I didn't have any supper yesterday."

The nurse went away to brush her hair and teeth, and to exchange slippers and kimono for a crisp white uniform and rubber-heeled shoes. Presently she went off downstairs, and when she came back she carried a tray with a white doily on it, and some of the best china, never used on ordinary occasions. The room was filled with the delicate fragrance of tea.

"I haven't had breakfast in bed for—why, it must be fifty years!" said Grandma. "Not since Frank was born. Frank was my younger son, you know—Harold's father. Why doesn't Harold come home? I want him to be here."

"Oh, I am sure he will come today some time," said the nurse in her best soothing technique—though of course she knew nothing at all about Harold or his whereabouts.

The whole business of being washed and of having her scanty white hair brushed and plaited for her delighted Grandma. How lovely it was to be waited on!

"I suppose there'll be people coming," said Grandma. "You'll find a piecework spread in the bottom drawer of the bureau—and my fascinator, please. The pillowcases are on a shelf of the linen closet, next to the bathroom. I want the ones with the embroidered monogram and the crochet edge."

The nurse—she was young and still expected people to follow accepted patterns of behavior—was scandalized. She thought her patient should have waked up to tears and moans, and here she was fussing about the set of the lavender knitted thing about her thin shoulders. Prettying up for company!

The nurse did not realize that, to the very old, death is so familiar an idea that it seems unimportant. The things that matter are to have hot tea and the best pillow slips while one still lives. Grandma Breen's mind was clear enough. She was perfectly aware that Will was probably dead, but it was a long time since he had been a solemn, curly-headed baby—her son. It was as though her son had died a long time ago. For years she had not felt the sonship of the hard, silent, aging man in this house. Harold had taken the place of son to her. She loved Harold.

The doorbell and the telephone began ringing before long. The nurse was kept in a marathon, running up and down stairs, till Mrs. Paradise arrived and took over the bells. People brought flowers, and glasses of crabapple jelly, ice cream, pitchers of buttermilk, jigsaw puzzles, and more flowers. They talked in whispers at the door or came up-stairs on tiptoe to look in a moment at the old woman, whose shrunken body hardly raised the gay print sunbursts of the piecework quilt, and whose waxy old face, incredibly small and still, lay against the blue-white of the best pillow slips.

"Mrs. Arthur Breen, known to all in Keedora as 'Grandma' Breen, aged mother of the missing banker, William Breen, whose mysterious disappearance some time after noon yesterday, July 27, has thrown an entire community into a condition of horror difficult to describe, lies prostrated by grief in the Breen mansion on Fifth Street."

So began Wally Price's article for the Chicago paper, all neatly typed, that rested in his coat pocket. He called in on his way to the airmail to ask at the door for the latest word on Grandma Breen's condition.

"Go right up and see her," Mrs. Paradise permitted; so Wally was among those who tiptoed and peered.

Grandma Breen might be dead, lying there, except for her eyes. Dark, brilliant, they shone out of the waxy-white mask of her face as alive as the eyes of a squirrel. They gave Wally a shock.

"Why!" he thought as he tiptoed hastily away," she isn't 'grief-stricken' at all! The old girl's having the time of her life."

It would never do, though, to say that in print. People would not like it. How conventional we are! It is the custom to pull a long face and talk in whispers in the presence of death. Of course some tears are real enough, and grief may be like looking into the darkness of hell. But to bystanders death is exciting. We—like it. *Macabre!* Grandma Breen was macabre. Wally was pleased with the word and wished he dared put it into his copy, but of course he couldn't. He slipped his manuscript, as it was, through the airmail slot in the post office.

Of course William Breen was dead. Everybody seemed to be taking that for granted. But what a grim joke on the community he had so profoundly thrilled by his disappearance if he were to return, alive and well! People, Wally reflected, wouldn't like that at all. He thought with comfort of Tina. If Wally Price were to disappear there would be at least one person to feel sorry.

Thinking of Tina reminded him of what she had said the night before—about the man who looked "queer," and who worked at Hathaway's garage. Of course there was no reason to connect the man with William Breen, but it wouldn't do any harm to go and look at him.

The only man he found at Hathaway's was Jeffers. Jeffers was a tall, bony something in greasy overalls, washing a car. Wally knew Jeffers in a way—as he knew every man, woman, child, and dog in Keedora. Jeffers was terribly thin, of course, but he looked perfectly ordinary to Wally.

Wally said he wanted his spark plugs tested. He had to say something.

"Didn't I see you out at the crossroads last night?" Wally suggested.

"I was out there," Jeffers answered.

"I guess pretty near everyone in Keedora was there."

"And no tears shed."

The man's tone was so strange that Wally pricked up his ears. Perhaps after all there was something in that hunch of Tina's.

"What do you suppose made them all go out there?" Wally said innocently.

"They kind of hoped they might see somebody that'd been shot or had a knife stuck in him."

"Is that why you went?"

"No. I saw all the corpses I'd care to—in the Argonne."

"Of course," exclaimed Wally with a flash of memory—a meeting in the high-school auditorium years ago, some men in uniform, somebody reading something out of a paper—" why, you're Captain Jeffers. I was there when they pinned the medal on you."

"A medal!" said Jeffers, with deep disgust.

"Well, if you didn't want to see a dead man, why—"

"Maybe I wanted to—not shed tears."

"You knew Mr. Breen?"

The man raised his eyes, and in them Wally saw something that turned him a bit sick. Hate. He had heard about hate. He had never seen it eye to eye before. Not like that.

The man turned back to his work.

"I knew Will Breen," he said quietly. "Your spark plugs are all right. What you need is to have the valves ground— and about a hundred other little things. Would hardly pay you."

He went back to the car dripping on the washing-rack.

Wally drove next to Bud Carson's filling station. Bud seemed to be doing a land-office business. A boy was helping him and both pumps were working. Cars driving in and driving away in a steady stream. Wally waited for some time before there was a short lull and he could get a word with Bud.

"Sold more gas already today than all last week," said Bud.

He looked hot and greasy, and very well pleased with the turn of events.

"How come?" Wally wanted to know.

"Oh, just a bunch of sensation-seekers, out to see if they can't pick up a thrill or two. It's good for business."

He wiped his damp face with an oily handkerchief.

"Harold Breen stopped here for gas yesterday, didn't he?" asked Wally.

Bud gave him a startled look.

"I got nothing to say about that," he insisted. "Here comes another bunch of cars; I got to get busy."

Wally lingered for a time, but he could get nothing out of Bud. The sheriff had probably warned him not to talk.

Giving it up as a bad job, he drove out toward Deland.

He stopped at the bridge to watch the citizens in boots, and the citizens with bare shanks, still wading about hopefully in the shallow river. As his luck was in, that day, he happened to be on hand when the spade was found. It was a quite ordinary spade. No one ever identified it positively, though several farmers of the district thought they might have had an old spade like that lying around. There were, of course, no fingerprints on it other than those of the enthusiastic finders; so it proved nothing, and was of no value as a clue, but people crowded about to look at it with shuddering awe. It might have been the spade used for a hurried and unholy burial; of course also it might not—but nobody cared to think about that.

The spade was carried, in great excitement, to the sheriff's office. For months it might have been seen there, standing in a corner against the wall. Perhaps it is still there. Mrs. Belinda Blum, the Woman's Club poetess, wrote a sonnet to it, beginning:

> O implement of honest, useful toil,
> To what dread use hast thou been put, alas!

She sent the poem to the *Bugle* and it appeared, in a neat box of black lines, in the middle of the editorial page on the day of the great mass-search for the "corpus delicti," and was later copied by many papers all over the country. So it was to William Breen that Mrs. Blum owed her literary triumph. She later delivered a paper on "The Art of Poesie" before the Woman's Club in which she explained just why she had decided on "implement of honest, useful toil" rather than "honest implement of useful toil" or "useful implement of honest toil." It made a very profound impression.

CHAPTER 9

SHERIFF FLAGLER was on his way to what he called "home"—a room in Mrs. Stark's boardinghouse on Second Street—at about the time Milly Slater and Grandma Breen were waking up. He felt very weary, and sad, and old. The daybreak clamor of the birds distressed him.

He wondered if Mrs. Stark had thought to leave a snack for him on the kitchen table, as she sometimes did when he had to be out late. He could do with a sandwich and a glass of cold milk. He fitted his key in the lock and let himself into the sleeping house, making as little noise as a large, tired man might be expected to make.

The hall was dark, but he noted with surprise as he groped his way toward the back of the house that a line of light showed under the kitchen door. In the kitchen he found the landlady asleep in the rocker with her head on the table.

She roused as he came in.

"I just couldn't go to bed," she explained, rubbing the sleep out of her eyes. "My! Ain't it awful! Have you caught him yet?"

"Caught—him?"

"Why, the murderer, of course."

"If there's been a murder," said the sheriff, "nobody knows it yet—except one. And he isn't telling. Will Breen may turn up today as alive as ever, wondering what all the excitement's about."

"Oh! Do you think so?"

Her tone was one of disappointment rather than relief.

"Let's hope so, anyway."

He sat down heavily at the table and lifted the napkin thrown over the plate of sandwiches.

Mrs. Stark bustled to the ice chest for a bottle of milk. She was an angular, acid person, engaged in a perpetual warfare against dust, flies, and bills. She had few pleasures in life, the sheriff reflected tolerantly. You could not blame her for getting a kick out of a real-life mystery in the neighborhood. She was a voracious reader of detective thrillers, and often discussed with her star boarder the fine points of the latest sample from the lending library. *The Murder at Murgytroid Mansions* lay open, face down, on the kitchen table where she had put it when sleep overcame her.

In fiction, the sheriff reflected, it is always the most improbable person who turns out in the end to have done the deed of darkness. But in real-life crime it is just the other way. If a woman is killed, find the husband; if a man is killed, it's the wife, or failing a wife the next of kin. Very depressing. The sheriff hated crime the way a good mechanic hates grit in the lubricating oil. He didn't hate criminals. Mostly they were just stupid people in a jam. But he wished they wouldn't act the way they did.

"I saw that Milly Slater downtown yesterday," Mrs. Stark was saying." She looked real peaked. If you ask me, she's in the family way. That Breen boy, of course. What the young people are coming to, these days!"

The sheriff did not answer, though her words startled and shocked him. He pushed his plate away and got his weary body up out of the chair.

"Well, good night to you, Mrs. Stark," he said, "and thank you for the lunch."

"Now, I do declare," cried the landlady, "you're that aggravating, Sheriff Flagler! With you right here in the house I don't know no more than everybody else!"

"Nobody knows anything yet," he said. "There's no use talking about it too much."

Mrs. Stark tossed her head and, picking up the half-empty milk bottle, stalked out to the ice chest on the back porch. Her back expressed her disappointment.

The sheriff stumbled off upstairs to bed. He needed the few hours' sleep he intended to allow himself.

But for some time he could not sleep. He lay and watched the window turn from gray torose, to gold, to full daytime brilliance. Damn it all! This Harold Breen, now—a good type of youngster, Harold. He hoped to God the young fellow would come off clear, but things looked bad. Motive enough, probably; time checked, unless Bud Carson was lying—and why should he lie? Next of kin, except for Grandma Breen, and of course she could be counted out.

It was going to be tough, arresting the boy, working up the evidence, seeing him brought to trial, perhaps to the chair. Would finish the old lady as surely as a knife in her heart. Grandma Breen thought the world and all of that boy. Well, it was there to be done. Murder is murder. And if Harold Breen said good-bye to Milly Slater, as she said, before eleven o'clock and then waited around for an hour to follow his uncle out of town, as Bud Carson's testimony seemed to show, why, it looked like deliberate murder.

Well, he reflected, maybe the young fellow had made his getaway. And before there could be a trial there'd have to be a "corpus delicti—" He slept at last.

Of all the people in Keedora, not even excepting Grandma Breen, nobody felt as great and genuine distress over the disappearance of Banker Breen as the good sheriff.

CHAPTER 10

KEEDORA WAS THRILLED at breakfast time to find itself on the front pages of city papers.

"I guess the whole country will be 'Keedora-conscious,' before night," said the secretary of the Keedora Chamber of Commerce to his wife. "A hundred thousand dollars' worth of advertising and not a cent to pay."

"Mr. Breen is paying, isn't he?" said Mrs. Secretary.

"Well, he is—at that. It's sort of ironic. He wouldn't give us a cent for our 'Come to Keedora' campaign we wanted to put on last spring."

"But what good can this kind of 'advertising' do?" She pointed over Mr. Secretary's shoulder to the black headline: "Prominent Mid-West Banker Disappears. Probably Slain or Kidnaped." Do you call that 'advertising'?"

"Sure it is. It makes people read and they find out it happened at Keedora. 'Keedora?' they say; 'now where is Keedora? Why, it's that place Tom So-and-So was talking about—thriving little town, shipping-point for hogs and grain, cheap power—I'll have to make that burg on my next trip." He comes and has a look around. Other people come. Anything that brings people here is good advertising. And this will bring them."

"I don't see why," said Mrs. Secretary slowly. "Oh, I suppose I do see why, but it's sort of horrible."

"Just human nature, my dear. We all like a touch of horror now and then—if it doesn't come too close."

He kissed his wife, grabbed his Panama, and went off downtown, feeling the springs of boosterism and ballyhoo renewed within him. Of late it had sometimes come a little hard to appear always bursting with enthusiasm for Keedora and Keedora's rosy future.

The whole town was astir. The first of the tourist procession were rolling in, to stop at some gasoline station for gas and directions.

"Gas?"

"Give me ten. And say, feller, whereabouts was this here banker murdered—or whatever happened to him?"

"Go right out along highway twenty-one. He stopped here for gas at eleven-thirty and started for Deland; but he never got there. That's about all anybody knows, yet."

A dozen times Bud Carson had spoken his little piece. Already it had become stereotyped. Money jingled into the cash register at a rate that made him rub his hands. He'd have to telephone right away for another tank car to come out on the midnight freight. . . .

Jessie Dean called in at the New York Store to ask Mrs. Minkler to hold that dress for her, after all.

"I've got a job for a few days," she explained. "Yes, at the telephone company. So many calls coming through they've got to have extra help on the switchboard."

Jessie Dean's heart sang. She needed that dress for the dance next Saturday. It would, she thought, give Joe Prince just that last push needed to take him over the hurdle of a proposal. She began planning where they would live when she was Mrs. Prince. Joe was making enough so they could get married right away—

Mattie Ellis got a job, too, answering the telephone in the office of the Keedora *Bugle*. A parrot or a phonograph record would have served as well:

"No, he hasn't been found yet. Terrible. All the news was in the morning paper. Yes, there'll be an extra this afternoon if they find him."

She hoped her voice would hold out. A good thing she'd thought to stop at the drug store for a box of those pastilles. The job probably wouldn't last very long, but even a day's pay—what a mercy! She'd be able to pay Mr. Laubesheimer a few dollars on his bill, and maybe get a steak for the children's supper.

"Bugle office. No, ma'am, he hasn't been found yet."

Lord! How long was it since they'd had a steak? Must be three months.

"Bugle office. No, sir, he hasn't been found yet. . . ."

The Bon-Ton Restaurant was doing a tremendous business. Greek Joe had had to send out twice already for more hamburger.

Cars traveled slowly along the road to Deland, the occupants hanging out of the lowered windows scanning the bushes and ditches in the horrid hope of seeing—what? Some were rewarded at the bridge by being on hand at the dramatic moment when the spade was fished out of the water. Most saw nothing but the corn and the hot sunshine.

Housewives hung over back fences telling each other what a horrible thing had happened. It was too hot, anyway, to be in the kitchen. Later they would send Johnnie or Eva down to the store for a loaf of bread and a dozen cinnamon rolls.

People made business at the bank to cash small checks or make small deposits, and to gaze with awe at a closed door lettered, "William Breen, President. Private."

Mr. Vane, the cashier, found it difficult to keep his face set in the expression of calm gravity that the occasion seemed to demand of him. The bank's four remaining directors were in there behind the closed door, with the state bank examiner—hastily summoned last night—and the corporation's lawyer. They were engaged in making a quick check-up of the bank's assets. It was just possible—though of course no one who knew William Breen could possibly suspect—

"Yes, Mrs. Smith, a very terrible thing." He spoke in a hushed, funereal voice, drawing down the corners of his mouth and shutting his eyes for a moment. "Five dollars?

Will you have it in change or in a bill? No—no ransom notes have been received. We know no more than was in the papers this morning."

He was keeping his ear cocked for sounds from the president's office. He could make nothing of the vague rumble of voices.

"A terrible thing, Mr. Jones." He drew down the corners of his mouth and closed his eyes for a moment. It was a technique. "You wish to deposit seven dollars and fifty cents? Thank you; here is the deposit slip. We know nothing more than was in the papers."

Was William Breen at that moment on a train or an airplane on his way to unextraditable ease with a few hundred thousands of the bank's funds in a modest suitcase at his feet? Mr. Vane knew how it could have been done. He had worked out a perfect system years ago. Now, of course, it would be too late—for him. Why hadn't he done it first? He pretended he believed it was his moral uprightness that had prevented, but as a matter of fact he was afraid of airplanes and got desperately seasick even in a rowboat on the lake. Of such things are virtue made sometimes.

When the crowd in the bank thinned out toward noon, Mr. Vane closed his wicket and went to the door of the president's room. He listened for a moment to the voices inside and then rapped. As no one answered, he opened the door a crack and peered in.

"Oh, Vane. Come on in."

It was Mr. Garland who spoke. Mr. Garland was a leonine person with a mass of white hair of which he was very proud. He looked like an actor, but was in fact a retired manufacturer of overalls and one of the directors of the bank.

"It's all right, Vane," he said. "Of course it will take time to make a complete survey, but we know enough to know that no sum of importance has disappeared. It's a relief from the standpoint of the bank, but makes it pretty sure

Breen has been either kidnaped or murdered. I'm afraid the poor fellow is dead." His tone was cheerful.

Mr. Vane drew down the corners of his mouth and shut his eyes for a moment. It had become a habit.

"Of course nobody really suspected a fine man like Mr. Breen of—theft," he said.

"The hell they didn't!" said one of the other directors.

"Telephone the sheriff, will you, Vane?" said the white-haired Garland." Use the telephone in the directors' room so that the people out there in the bank won't hear. Just tell Flagler that we're pretty sure everything is straight here at the bank. . . ."

The sheriff sat at his battered desk and looked at the spade. The spade was a grim object. Looking at it did something to him. He looked up at the opening of the door.

"You doped it out right, Sheriff," reported the deputy who had come in. "Chief of police at Christian just called. Harold Breen wasn't with the bunch, though."

"Maybe they got the wrong outfit."

"Not a chance. Six young fellows crowded into a car with a lot of camping stuff. Headed for Pine Cone Lake. Said Harold Breen was to have met them at Des Moines around noon yesterday, but he didn't show up, and they got tired waiting so they started along. Figured he'd catch up when they camped for the night. But they ain't seen hide nor hair of him. Looks kind of bad."

The sheriff said nothing; but one of his big hands, lying on his desk, clenched into a fist.

"Think he did it—the young fellow? Bumped off Old Man Breen?"

"It's too soon, Mike. We won't say it yet but it looks bad as hell. We got to find this Harold Breen. Here's the description. Get it on the wires. And telephone the chief of police in Des Moines and get them to have it go out on the radio."

"You don't take much stock in that kidnaping talk Witherspoon's putting out over at Deland, do you, Sheriff?"

"Wish to God I did!" the sheriff sighed. "Mike, I'd give a thousand dollars to have this not happen. It's a bad business, any way you look at it. Tim back yet?"

"I'll go see."

The deputy went to the door and called into the outer office, "Tim back yet?"

The clerk at the desk called back over his shoulder, "Here he comes, now."

"All right, Mike. Get after that description. Make up a handbill, too, and take it over to the printer. Tell him to get all-fired busy on it. Sit down, Tim. Get anything?"

"Sure looks bad for young Breen, Sheriff," said Tim eagerly. "Found six people say they're ready to swear they saw Harold Breen around town about noon yesterday. Bud Carson says there can't be no mistake—it was about eleven-thirty when Will Breen stopped for gas, and Harold he came along about fifteen minutes later. A farmer by the name of Branch says he was driving into town and seen two cars parked at the top of the hill above the river. One of them was a black sedan. There was only one man, stooped over doing something with a jack under the back wheel of the sedan. Didn't see his face, but it couldn't 'a' been Breen because he had on a dark suit and one of these here fedora hats. And, say, here's a funny one! Kid that drives the milk-wagon for the CloverBloom outfit says he saw Harold Breen right out on Fifth Street this morning, about sunup. He knows young Breen, all right—went to high school with him. And he's sure it wasn't yesterday morning because he saw young Breen yesterday morning, too."

"Get hold of Branch and this kid and have them come in. Guess I'd better talk to them myself."

The sheriff's face looked old and weary.

"Hits the Old Man pretty hard," thought Tim. "Wonder why? No reason he should love Will Breen. Must be the young fellow. Sure, that's the answer. That boy of his sister's that the Old Man set such store by, and that got drowned last summer—he used to pal around a lot with this Harold Breen. Tough, all right, but it's him done it, sure as shooting. Hope he makes his getaway. That old skinflint needed killing."

CHAPTER 11

HAROLD WAS SINGING, in his sweet, boyish baritone against the rusty clack of the old motor as he and Milly drove westward through the milk-warm dawn. Corn-weather. It would be another day of burning heat.

"Don't you think we ought to keep to the back roads, Harold?" Milly asked.

"Afraid Uncle Will is going to come tearing after us?" laughed Harold. "Don't you worry. He can't do anything to stop us now. Besides, he thinks I'm up in Wisconsin by this time."

A trembling took the girl. Every time he spoke his uncle's name she felt a stab of fear. It was wrong not to tell him what had happened, but she must not tell. If she told, he would go back. And for her there could be no going back.

Something in her silence penetrated his uplifted mood. He took his eyes from the road for a glance at her. She was huddled in the far corner of the seat, and her eyes were dark and enormous in the dead-white oval of her face.

"Why, you are scared!" he said. "Gosh, Milly, we'll get along all right, even if Uncle Will doesn't come around. We've got enough money between us to take us clear to California if we want to go that far. I'll get a job. I'll take care of you. Why! you're crying!"

Milly tried to choke back her sobs, but they shook her—tore at her. She was stifled by them.

The boy was alarmed by the intensity of her emotion, that seemed to him entirely mysterious. He stopped the car at the side of the road under a tree and took her in his arms.

"Milly! Milly, dear! What is it? Look, if you're so frightened we'll go back. We'll wait."

"Oh! no," she cried. "Not that! We mustn't go back." By a great effort she got control of herself, sat up straight and dried her eyes. "See, Harold, I'm all right, now." She forced her stiff lips to smile.

He could not make her out at all. For weeks she had been urging him to take her away, and now he had done it—going against his uncle's wishes to do it—and she had to act like this! Girls! Who could understand them?

The sun, just coming up over the rim of the world, shone on the under sides of the branches of the tree above their heads in a theatrical effect that seemed unnatural and disquieting. The empty road stretched ahead with their shadows, grotesquely elongated, spread on its dusty and uneven surface. On either side marched the corn in its geometrical ranks from horizon to horizon.

"All right," he said at last, tight-lipped.

He turned away from her, back to the wheel, stepped on the starter and set the aged car in motion.

They went on for a long way in silence, past farms where the day's work was beginning—a man crossing a barnyard with a foamy pail of milk in each hand, a boy harnessing a team of enormous shaggy-hoofed horses to a wagon, a dog that barked after them for a short way, chickens that scuttled across the road—through bits of woodland; across sluggish ocher-colored creeks, glassy smooth between yellow clay banks.

The boy was no longer singing. He was feeling of a sudden oppressed by the huge indifference of the world, and thinking very soberly of his responsibility toward Milly. He had promised to take care of her; he wanted to make her happy. It might not be so easy.

Milly's fears were deeper and more concrete.

"We're coming to a town," he said. "I suppose this would be as good a place as any for us to stop and get married."

"Not yet," said Milly. "Not so near. Somebody might see us and know us. Besides, it's too early—we'd have to wake people up."

What difference would it make if people did see them? He wondered. But he said nothing. It was, of course, still too early. The wide street between the low buildings was empty; curtains were still drawn down and only a few chimneys showed a wisp of smoke where breakfast fires were being started. They slipped through the town without stopping.

The day wore on toward noon and the heat became stifling, even in the moving car. They came then to a patch of woodland; oaks and hickories and maples standing thickly together in a hollow between low hills. A little creek ran through the place.

Harold drove to the side of the road and stopped.

"I'm about all in," he said, "and I guess you are, too."

From the camp supplies in the back of the car he unpacked the makings of a clumsy, boyish meal and spread them on the grass beside the creek in the shade of a huge old tree. The setting was romantic and so, of course, was the situation, but Harold did not feel romantic. This was the hell of an elopement! Hot. Stifling even here under the trees. He thought of the cold little Wisconsin lake with its border of firs, a trout leaping. He ate.

Milly said she was not hungry. She sat in the long grass with her back against the rough bark of the tree. Her face, very little and white, was tipped back so that green lights played over it, caressing the delicate contours and outlining the round softness of her young throat. There was something futile and pathetic about her nerveless hand, lying open—palm upturned—in the grass beside her.

Harold did not see her as pathetic. What made her want to act like a sick cat? Hadn't he given up his vacation, thrown up his job at the bank, set his uncle against him, all for her? You'd think he was carrying her off against her will, the way she was acting. He bit angrily into a stale bun.

But, his hunger satisfied, he began to feel a little better. He lay down flat in the grass. It was pleasant here, out of the sun, with the gentle cool voice of the little stream in his ears, and not a single stalk of corn in sight. He spoke of that to Milly.

"The corn gets me down," he said. "There's so darn much of it; it's so inhuman, and so sort of human, too, all at the same time. It likes to be hot and it stands there in the sun and laughs at you, sweltering. We'll keep going till there isn't any more corn, anywhere. What do you say?"

"That would be—nice."

He was not looking at her. He did not see how pale she was or that her cheeks were wet.

"I wish I didn't feel the way I do about Uncle Will," he went on, thinking aloud. "He's looked after me since I was a kid, and I suppose he's done what he thought was best. But why couldn't he be a little different? Why did he have to make things so hard for us? I'll make him pay—some day."

The girl gave a little cry—"Oh! Don't!"

He sat up and looked at her. Then, "Milly! What's the matter?"

She was shaking like a leaf and her eyes were big and stary. She frightened him.

A wave of tenderness for her went over him—she was so little and scared and helpless.

"Milly, talk to me. Tell me what's the matter."

She told him then. She had to tell him.

He sat stunned for a minute.

"Uncle Will, gone. Perhaps murdered," he said slowly. "And you let me come away like this! Don't you see—they'll think I did it. Killed him."

"I was afraid," moaned the girl. "They'd have—"

"And Grandmother there, all alone!"

"But you didn't do it—and, there's something else. I had to get away. I just had to, Harold."

He didn't understand her.

"You let me sneak off like this and leave Grandmother alone with nobody to help her! Oh! how could you do that to me, Milly? We're going back. Now."

He sprang up and pulled her roughly to her feet.

"They'll—put you in prison."

"Oh, no, they won't! See here, you don't think I did something to Uncle Will, do you?"

She hung her head under his angry eyes. She knew he had had nothing to do with his uncle's disappearance, but for a minute—when the sheriff was talking to her—she had been afraid—

"Come along." He took her arm and hurried her roughly out to the road and the parked car. "When I think of Grandmother—" He choked.

"He would do more for his grandmother than he would for me," Milly thought. It was true, perhaps, but her thought was unfair just the same. "Even if I told him, now, he'd go back." Of course he had to go back.

Harold drove fast, back along the long way they had come. He kept his eyes straight ahead and paid no attention to Milly, huddled in her corner of the seat. She felt utterly lost. The jolting over the rutted country road made her giddy and the heat was terrific.

Behind the car trailed a long yellow roll of dust that hung for miles a few feet above the roadway as though beaten down and prevented from rising by the fierce rays of the sun. Dust was everywhere. For a distance on each side of the road there was no green—the grass in the ditches, the weeds along the fences, the overhanging trees, even the nearer ranks of corn, were all encrusted with yellow.

Milly breathed dust and felt it gritty in her mouth. It

caked the corners of her eyes. She thought, "Perhaps I am going to die," and hoped she might. But she was a long way from that.

Harold pulled up at last at a little country filling station. The gas tank was almost empty. Not far away ran two glimmering lines—the railroad, with a little red box of a country railroad station at the end of a short crossroad.

Harold had got out of the car to look at the oil gauge. Milly slipped out on the opposite side, making no sound, and turned away toward the station. She stumbled along in the dust as fast as she was able, but she had not got very far before Harold missed her and came striding after her. He took her roughly by the arm and spun her around.

"Milly! What in hell do you think you're doing!"

"I can't go back, Harold," she said, facing the fury of his dust-caked face and red-rimmed eyes. "I'm going— away. Let me go."

"Of course you're coming back." His fingers bit into the tender flesh of her arm and he felt her wince. "Are you crazy?"

She made a helpless little gesture with her free hand.

"Let me go," she said in a stifled voice. "You don't understand—"

But even now she could not tell him her secret. What good would it do to tell him now? He had to go back, in spite of anything. She saw that. But for her to go back meant—She could not face what it meant.

The faint hoot of a distant train came to them across the cornfields.

"The train's coming!" she cried. "You've got to let me go."

With a sudden wrench she tore herself free and started to run. It was a futile effort, for of course he caught her within a few strides.

"You're coming back if I have to drag you," he said

furiously. "You little fool—!"

He looked down into her face on which was the blank calmness of despair, and his anger went out of him. He dropped her arm.

"All right," she said dully, and turned back toward the car.

The man at the filling station looked at them curiously as they got in and drove away.

Keedora again. And again it was evening. Harold drew up in the side street, before the gate to the long garden. Milly got out. Her lips parted—she wanted to say something to Harold, but no words came. He kept his face resolutely turned away.

He was gone. Milly, holding herself upright against the gate, watched him turn the corner into Fifth Street. There was a pothole at the corner and he took it roughly, so that the loose equipment in the back of the car rattled. He did not look back. . . .

CHAPTER 12

MILLY OPENED THE GATE and let herself into the garden. She was not crying. She was far beyond tears. She sat for a long time on the bench under the lilacs while the daylight slowly faded. Big gray moths came out to hover over the dim flower beds where nightflowers were opening and sending out into the warm darkness their passionate fragrance—the essence of sweet, secret things. The evening star hung in the pale sky like a lamp, and fireflies came and went over the grass in a crisscross of tiny flashes. Children were running and laughing in the street and a woman's voice was calling: "Bernice! Ber*neece!*" over and over.

Milly was not thinking in any orderly, conscious way. Her mind held, not a procession of ideas each touching the one ahead, but a jumble of disconnected pictures—the white dress she wore for her graduation from high school; a dead bird lying on a pathway in the garden; a bangle with a little gold heart hanging from it that someone had given her for her tenth birthday; her stepfather's face as he leaned over to say good-bye to her that morning in the dark hall; a picture in a silly book she had been reading. Harold was in the pictures, but his face was a blank, as though rubbed out with an eraser, oval and smooth as an egg.

But she must think. There was something she must do. She tried to steady the dizzy whirl of her mind, but before she could catch an idea and hold it, others came crowding. And all the while with a part of her consciousness she was calmly aware of the evening, the fireflies, the children's voices.

Then, suddenly, she felt for the first time the stirring of a new life—that life unsanctioned by a paper with the county clerk's name on it, over which no one in a priestly robe had intoned words out of a book; that undesired new life, created of love and youth and impatience. She shut her eyes and clung to the back of the bench and for a moment everything went black. She was floating in a sea of blackness—

When she came to herself again, her mind had cleared. She knew now what it was she must do. Money. She would need money. Yes, the roll of bills her stepfather had pressed into her hand that morning was still in her handbag.

At the house no one was expecting her. She saw the house through the shrubbery, a dark bulk against the evening sky. The window of her room; dark. A light was burning in the dining room, and against the yellow rectangle of the window she saw silhouetted the graceful sprays of the rose vine from which Harold had broken the rose that roused her in the dawn. Someone was running the water in the kitchen and she heard the clash of dishes; supper must be over. She was reminded that she had eaten nothing since the day before, but she felt no hunger for food. She wished Jim were here with her in the dark garden; the touch of his hand would have been a comfort. But of course that could not be.

At the foot of the street ran a streetcar line, but when the car came along, it was blazing with lights and crowded with people, riding for the breeze on this hot night. Milly did not stop it. She would have to walk.

It was a long way, on foot, to the place where she was going—all across town, past the brickyard and the gasworks, past the Lutheran Church where the praying and preaching were done in German. She had gone there one Sunday when she was a small child, with a German maid. She could remember the stuffy smell and the glare of the bare windows. . . .

Then along badly lighted streets whose mean little wooden boxes of houses stood farther and farther apart, with weedy tangles of wasteland between, till they stopped altogether in a region of eroded clay banks and tin cans. After that, open country with cornfields, aglitter in the moonlight.

Milly came to the house. It stood back from the road at the end of a neglected driveway with the moonlight full in its dismal face. Milly had not been afraid of the summer dark—she was afraid of the house. It had a tower with dead eyes and a naked flagstaff. It had many tall, narrow windows and a black cavern of porch in the depths of which was the door through which she would have to pass. The jigsaw woodwork of the porch was broken, and the steps sagged forlornly into a lawn where the uncut grass stood high and stiff. An iron stag, leprous with scaly patches of rust, stood at bay in the shrubbery.

In daylight the place was grotesque, but by night—and if one knew what happened under its ugly mansard roof—it was sinister enough.

Milly, in a daze of weariness, misery, and fear, stumbled up the steps as so many young, unhappy things had done before her, and pressed her finger on the white button of an electric bell.

CHAPTER 13

ON THAT STICKY-HOT NIGHT, when most of the people in Keedora were out-of-doors, fanning themselves in the screened darkness of their porches or looking for a breeze with their cars along the country roads, five men lingered about an untidy table in the dining room of the Keedora Hotel.

A droning electric fan stirred the stale air into whirls without producing any sense of refreshment, serving merely to mix together the smells of cold gravy, stale coffee grounds and coarse vegetables, with an occasional hot whiff of dishwater from the kitchen.

In spite of two violently green artificial palms in tubs and a listless canary in a dangling gilt cage the dining room of the Keedora Hotel was hardly a spot for agreeable dalliance; but the men at the corner table were so deep in their discussion that they had not noticed the departure of the last diner or the closing of the double doors leading to the lobby.

Miss Brill, the angular head waitress, was all aflutter with excitement under her stiffly starched uniform. She hovered over her little desk by the door pretending to be busy with menu cards and little slips of paper, but straining her ears for scraps of the fascinating conversation. All that reached her were tag ends of sentences, a word here and there, all confused in the whirring of the fan. Dignity of position prevented her from drawing close and listening frankly like Etta, the waitress who stood beside the serving table with her mouth hanging open and her eyes popping. Some people have all the luck.

The man doing the talking was Bob Grant, star reporter of a big St. Louis paper. He flicked the ashes of his cigarette into the muddy dregs of his last cup of coffee and announced that as far as he was concerned the story was a flop, and that unless something broke before midnight he intended to hop the twelve-twenty out. He was a chunky, sandy-colored person who would have been the better for a shave and a course of clothespressing and shoe-shining.

"A wash-out," he declared in tones of disgust. "I ask you! No ransom note, no corpse. They haven't even found his car. For all we know the bird's just gone fishing, or done an elopement with his cook. What the cash customers want with their breakfast bacon is blood, and lots of it—or at least a little torture."

Wally Price, thrilled and more than a little awed by the distinguished company in which he found himself, stuttered with eagerness.

"But"—he urged—"something's happened to him, sure. Mr. Breen—why, he's one of those people, never a minute late in his life, never half a beat off. Like clockwork. He wouldn't—"

"Oh, sure," agreed Grant, "some egg's probably bumped the old geezer off, all right. But what does that get us if there isn't a corpse? Might hang around here a month without finding anything to wire in about except the weather." He mopped his face with a damp handkerchief. "Say, it's hotter here than in St. Louis!"

Wally Price felt balked. The crime was in a way his crime and it hurt him to have it misprized. His eyes traveled anxiously around the table.

Matter, of the Kansas City *American,* leaned an elbow on the untidy cloth and stared dreamily at nothing. It was impossible to tell what he was thinking. He was a long, stringy young man with a small smudge of black mustache between his long, pale nose and his full, red lips. Hair a little too long, picturesquely disordered. Poetic type. He was smoking a Russian cigarette as thin as a match with an air of gentle melancholy.

Raines, the camera man from Chicago, appeared placidly unconcerned. His not to reason why, his merely to shoot here and there as occasion and his partner suggested. His only contribution to the symposium was the occasional sharp little snap of a nutshell between the jaws of the nutcracker he was wielding.

But when Wally's eyes got around to Jones, of the Chicago *Record-Herald,* they found a ray of hope. Jones, solid, dynamic, was puffing at a fat torpedo-shaped cigar. His expression was alert, interested.

Wally felt that here was someone who believed in the famous crime and found it worthwhile.

"How about you, Matter?" Grant was saying. "Going to beat it out with me on the twelve-twenty?"

"Guess I'll stick around another day, anyhow," said Matter in his lazy drawl. "Might work up something on the kidnaping angle."

"Horse-feathers!" said Grant. "That Sheriff Witherspoon over in Deland is just romancing to get his name in print. He never saw Lefty Magoon—nor any other big-time gangster—around Deland."

"Sure, he's grandstanding," said Matter indifferently. "But aren't we all?"

"Got a check-up on Magoon," said Jones, around his cigar. "Magoon's spotted in Tucson, so that's out."

"We haven't tried the suicide angle," suggested Matter. "This Breen, now—maybe he's been juggling with bank funds and takes himself off into the bushes and gives himself a shot of cyanide. Or maybe he's taken a run-out powder, with a fat package of collateral in his briefcase—"

"Suicide!" Grant snorted. "A lot of kick there is in suicide without any sex interest! And who's going to get all excited reading about a few dollars maybe missing from a hick bank?"

"Of course, Matter, you're talking through your hat to get Grant all in a lather," said Jones amiably. "But something down here looks worthwhile to you. What is it? Spill it, guy."

Matter flicked the ash from his cigarette with a manicured fingernail. "You're right, Jones," he said. "I am interested in a way. The 'human interest' thing."

" 'Human interest'! Human poppycock!" Grant's tone was sarcastic. "Where's the big heartthrob, I ask you, in anything that could have happened to a human adding machine like this Breen? As far as I can find out there isn't a soul in town that owes him anything but money and spite. How about it, kid?" He turned to Wally.

"People don't—didn't—like Mr. Breen very well," admitted Wally. "But, of course, he's prominent here in Keedora and around. He was a state senator once, you know."

"State senator! My hat!" jeered Grant.

"Let's hear about it, Matter," prompted Jones.

Matter twiddled with his glass and for a minute no one spoke. The canary gave an indignant chirp. It was long past his time to be left in darkness and quiet. The electric fan droned on. Not a breath of air came through the open windows, between the faded liver-colored "drapes." In the light from the dining room the sauntering summer-night feet of Keedora's citizens might be glimpsed briefly as they passed along the pavement outside. The dining room was below the street level and only feet and calves were visible, sauntering across the upper half of the windows.

"It isn't Breen, of course," said Matter slowly." It's the town. The way the town takes the thing. Excitement. A break in the monotony. Something for the women to say 'Oh!' and 'Ah!' about to each other over back fences while the bread burns in the oven. Telephones ringing. Telephone company's had to put two extra girls on the switch-

board. Know what a few days' work means to those girls? I
do—lunched with one of them today. Tourists—plenty of
them—coming through instead of going 'round by Depew.
What for? Just a ride out along the road to Deland and gape
at the cornfields and wonder where 'it' happened. Gasoline. Fellow at the filling station told me he'd sold twice as
much gas today and yesterday as all last week. Hot dogs.
Ice-cream cones. Tourists eat. New money in most of the
cash registers in town."

" 'Stone-thrown-into-stagnant-pool' kind of thing," said
Grant unpleasantly.

"More like 'yeast in the home brew,' " said Matter." Dull
lives. Starved for something to make the blood run faster
and make the ideas foam a bit. Stalwart citizens in boots
getting a great kick out of wading up and down that thin
little river, in water not deep enough to hide a dead chip-
munk—looking for a corpse. People walking around in the
woods and fields instead of rotting in stuffy rooms. Everybody looking for a corpse. Exciting!"

"Funny, in a horrible kind of way," Matter went on.
"Pathetic, too. And maybe a little dangerous."

"Did you see old lady Breen?" Jones laughed. "All
fussed up in lavender and lace, propped up in bed with
about a hundred women milling 'round, having the time
of her life."

"Trained nurse and best pillow slips, a whole flower
garden in jugs on the dresser," said Matter. "Yes, I saw her."

"I shot her three times," said the camera man. "She was
particular to be shot from the left side; she said that side of
her face was better looking than the other." He munched
another almond.

"And underneath it all," said Matter, "there's a
drama—something we don't know about. Somebody with
enough hate or enough greed or something to put Breen
on the spot. Probably somebody right here in Keedora,

going on about his business, feeling—how? Scared? Trium-
phant? The story's there all right—" His lazy voice trailed
off into silence.

A girl's laugh drifted in from the street. A pair of high
heels accompanied by a pair of masculine white sport shoes
went across the top of the window.

"Most people think Harold Breen did it," said Wally.
"But he's a good kid—"

"Might be anybody," said Matter. "The wish to kill is a
perfectly natural thing. We all have it."

"There's something about murder, all right," said Jones
reflectively. "Everybody likes to read about it. A safe way to
work off the impulse, I suppose."

"Nuts!" said Grant. He took a toothpick from the con-
tainer in the center of the table, stuck it in his mouth, and
got to his feet. "When you flush this 'hidden drama' of
yours, Matter, don't forget to sprinkle salt on its tail. Me—
I'm on my way. I suppose you're staying on, Jones?"

"Guess I'll stick here another day, anyhow," said Jones.
"Matter's got me interested."

Miss Brill unlocked the door and they all trooped out of
the dining room together.

"My! Miss Brill," said Etta, round-eyed with excitement,
"isn't he just wonderful!"

"If you mean the one with the Charlie Chaplin mustache," said Miss Brill, tossing her head, "I can't say I agree
with you."

"But he's so romantic!" sighed Etta. "And he talks just
like a book."

"He never even knew you were around," said Miss Brill
cruelly. "You'd better be getting those dishes out into the
kitchen or Oscar'll be wild."

"Oscar!" said Etta, with disdain.

And so Oscar's budding romance was blighted. He
wouldn't, he said, grow a little trick mustache for anybody,

and he'd have felt like a fool, "talking like a book," even if he'd known how. The children Oscar and Etta might have had were never born, and here was one of the incalculable "angles" of Banker Breen's taking-off that may—who knows?—have affected the history of the world. Though that is hardly likely.

CHAPTER 14

"YOU SAY," said the sheriff, his keen blue eyes on the youngster sitting before him with bowed head, "that you came back this morning to get Milly Slater and elope with her, and that she didn't tell you about what had happened till you stopped at noon. And that then you came right back."

"That's the truth, sir," said the boy. "I wouldn't have run away. I haven't done anything."

"How came you to come back here instead of going up north with those boys, the way you planned?"

"Well, I was late getting started. I got to Des Moines, but the others had gone on. I kept thinking all the time about Milly, so after a while I turned around and came back."

"What time did you get back?"

"I don't know exactly. It was still kind of dark. Milly heard me in the garden and came out."

"Anyone else hear you?"

"Mr. Gordon did—or anyway he heard Milly. He talked to her. He gave her some money. Her mother didn't wake up."

"You and Milly stop anywhere and get yourselves married?"

"I wanted to stop at the first town we came to, but Milly acted scared. She wanted to get farther away."

"What did you do with Milly when you got back?"

"Why, I took her home, of course."

"Your uncle, I take it, didn't want you should get married. You're over twenty-one, aren't you?"

"Uncle Will was my guardian, and wouldn't let me have the money my father left me. According to the will he had the say-so till I got to be twenty-five."

"People hadn't ought to make wills," said the sheriff. "This money, now, what shape was it in? Where was it? How much was there?"

"All I know is that it was in bonds. I don't know exactly how much it is now, with the interest, and with the money for my education taken out. It's in a box at the bank. Uncle Will showed it to me once."

"Never suspicioned that maybe it might not be there any more?" The sheriff eyed the boy keenly, and noted with satisfaction his start of shocked surprise.

"Why—!" The boy swallowed convulsively." Uncle Will wouldn't—! I don't believe it."

"'Fraid you'll have to," said the sheriff. "Been checking up over at the bank. The money's gone. Your uncle took care of you, though, after a fashion. When he—borrowed—the bonds he took out an insurance policy to cover, and if he's dead you won't be the loser. Sure you didn't know about it?"

"So that's why—!" The boy did not trouble to answer the question. He hardly heard it.

"Yes. That's why he couldn't let you get married and have your money. He was in a tight place, seems like."

"I wish he'd told me," said the boy.

"You and Milly been going together quite a while, I hear."

"Yes. We've been engaged for more than a year."

"Milly isn't—well, going to have a baby, is she?"

"Of course not." The boy's face reddened; he started up." I don't see what right—!"

"Steady, son. I just wanted to know. Now, here's some more things I want to know: Grandma Breen says you started off on this fishing trip right early—what time you figure you left town?"

"Why—I stopped to say good-bye to Milly. She didn't want me to go. She wanted me to take her away. Elope. We talked a long time. You know how it could be."

"Where was this? At her place?"

"No. We wanted to be by ourselves, so we drove out to the Spring. It was pretty late when we got back, so I didn't take her home. I let her out at the cemetery and she went home on the streetcar. She'd been crying. I kept thinking about that."

"What time was all this?"

"Must have been close to noon."

"Milly told me it was around ten-thirty or quarter to eleven when you left her at the cemetery."

He had come to the point of his questioning.

"I thought what you wanted to know was what time I left town," said the boy, coloring uncomfortably under the sheriff's searching eyes. "I—I drove a little way out of town and got to thinking about Milly. Crying. I turned around and went back. I drove up to her house and went into the garden and called up to her —her room has a window on the garden—but she didn't answer. I don't know where she was."

Milly had been lying on her bed, with her head buried in the pillow, sobbing her heart out, but he did not know that.

"I stood there in the garden a while, and then I said, "Oh, to hell with it!" and went away again. Bud Carson can tell you when I left town if you don't believe me. I stopped to fill my gas tank."

"He's already told me, son. You left town, according to Bud, about fifteen minutes after your uncle. Talk straight. I think you have, so far. Did you see your uncle on the road?" He shot the question at the boy, hard, like a blow.

Harold hesitated a moment, and then defiantly, "Yes, I saw him. What about it?"

"That's what I want to know."

"He'd stopped beside the road at the top of the hill

above the river. Had a flat. He was out there in the sun working on it. I pulled up and went to help him, but he snapped at me—wanted to know why I wasn't most to Des Moines by that time, and a lot of other stuff. It made me mad. If I'd stayed I'd have said something, so I just turned around and got back into my bus and drove away."

"You sure that's how it was?"

"That's exactly how it was. I didn't—do anything to Uncle Will. I—he—we didn't get along very well sometimes, but he'd looked after me all my life. I—You believe me, don't you, Mr. Flagler?"

The sheriff took the cigar out of his mouth and looked at it meditatively, as though he had never seen such an object before.

"Yes, son," he said at last. "I believe you. But it isn't sure other people will. The county attorney, I mean. It's got to be worked out. Think you could find the place—the exact spot—where you saw your uncle changing the tire?"

"I'm sure I could." The boy started up. "Can we go now?"

"Guess we'll wait till daylight. We'll go out there first thing in the morning."

"What do you think happened to Uncle Will, Sheriff? A person can't just disappear—"

"Well, Harold, we don't know much yet. We know he didn't run off with money from the bank. We checked that. He may have committed suicide, though that don't seem hardly likely. He wasn't that kind, and though he was hard-pressed some ways for money, it wasn't that bad. We figure somebody met him there on the road. A farmer that was driving by says he saw two cars parked at the top of the hill. Witherspoon over in Deland thinks maybe it's a kidnaping, but there's no ransom notes. You able to think of anybody might have had a grudge against your uncle?"

"You mean—that might have killed him?" The boy's

face paled. "You think it's—Murder?"

"Well, what else could it be, son?" the sheriff said. "It don't seem hardly likely he'd just go away like that without letting your grandma or anybody know. Of course maybe that's exactly what he's done—for some reason of his own that we can't dope out. We'll kind of hope, anyway, that that's how it was. I guess that's all now, youngster. You go home to your grandma and get yourself a night's sleep. You look like you need it. In the morning you and I'll take a run out the road and see what we can find."

 CHAPTER 15

IT WAS WALLY PRICE'S good luck to be in the hallway when Harold came out of the sheriff's office. Otherwise the avid readers of next morning's papers might not have learned at breakfast of the young man's return.

"What did young Breen have to say for himself, Sheriff?" Wally burst into the office to ask.

"Well, now, be reasonable, Wally," the sheriff protested. "If it was anything important would I be likely to hand it to you to be spread out in print?"

"But, Mr. Flagler, this thing means a lot to me—maybe a job, and everything—"

"It sort of means quite a lot to Harold, too," the sheriff pointed out dryly.

"You didn't arrest him?"

"What would I arrest him for? We don'tknow yet that anything's happened to arrest anybody for."

"Well—of course there's no 'corpus delicti,' but—"

"That's about the size of it. No 'corpus delicti' whatsoever, and no black sedan. You find those little things for us, and—"

"Look here, Sheriff," said Wally, "this town's all in a stew. Nobody liked Will Breen, but to have him knocked off like that kind of gets everybody all worked up. In the heat, and everything. They'll say you ought to have locked up Harold Breen."

"Sure they will, but what of it?" The sheriff's eyes were stern.

"Haven't forgotten, have you, that there's an election coming off? Oh, now, don't get mad, Sheriff. They say if you don't do something pretty quick they will, and—"

"Well, Wally, I'm aiming to give them all they want in

the way of doing. Put it in your paper if you like. If Will Breen ain't found before Sunday—that's day after tomorrow—we're all going out and look for him. The whole town. Everybody. There won't be a foot of ground between here and Deland that isn't gone over thorough."

"Hot dog!" cried Wally, his eyes shining.

"That's the old fight! 'Corpus delicti,' here we come!"

"Of course," said the sheriff, "it ain't certain there is any 'corpus delicti,' and even if there is, a fellow that had one to get rid of might travel a hundred miles or more before he'd pick him a likely spot."

Wally's enthusiasm was considerably dashed.

"You couldn't cover that much territory in a year," he complained. "If it's like that, why do you do it at all?"

"There's a chance we might find something, and anyhow it'll give the town something to do besides talk. Here's a tip for you, Wally—lay off young Breen."

"You mean—he didn't do it?" Wally blinked.

Mentally he was going over his "story," ready typed in his pocket, to change the slant of some of the phrases. As they stood, they seemed to spell Harold Breen.

"But about this corpse-hunt, now—going to put somebody special in charge, and all that?"

"Of course," said the sheriff. "There's a Captain Jeffers, ex-service man, works down at Hathaway's garage—Say, know anything about Jeffers?" Wally had given a start at the name and a queer look had come over his open face.

"Got all decorated up about something while I was in high school," said Wally.

The sheriff studied Wally through half-closed eyes. The kid had some kind of hunch in connection with Jeffers.

"Where'll I find this Jeffers bird?" said Wally, getting to his feet. "Got to get some dope on the big hunt right away."

"He's going to use the office of the Keedora Realty Company tomorrow—Gordon said he could let him have desk room, and use of all his big-scale maps."

"I mean, where'll I find him tonight? This dope's got to be pushed through for the morning editions."

"Couldn't say. Call Hathaway, maybe he can tell you."

"Well, thanks for everything, Sheriff. I've got to step on it."

Wally snatched up his hat and departed in a rush.

After Wally was gone, the sheriff sat for some time thinking over his talk with Harold Breen. The boy, he believed, had told the truth. Farmer Branch had not been able to describe the second parked car with any particularity, but he was very positive it was not a roadster with the top down and a lot of camping equipment loaded on the back. He thought he had passed a car like that just as he left Deland, but he could not be certain. It all checked pretty well.

The sheriff thought over, too, the talk he had had with Jeffers, and pondered the odd expression on Wally Price's face.

Jeffers was, as usual, sluicing down a car on the washing-rack when the sheriff sought him out.

"Hathaway's willing to spare you for a day or two, Jeffers," he had said, "and I believe you, with your army training, could handle this thing the way it's got to be handled."

Jeffers did not answer for a minute.

"I could do it," he said at last, "but maybe you know—and maybe you don't—that there's probably nobody in Keedora that hates Will Breen the way I hate him."

"No. I didn't know you knew him."

"I knew him, all right." The tone was bitter. "Of course I'd just as lief find his body, but don't count on me to help catch whoever did it—I'd like to shake that man's hand."

CHAPTER 16

JIM GORDON came down to breakfast late. He usually did. It was not laziness, but a profound despair that made getting up to begin a new day an act requiring a supreme marshaling of courage each morning.

As usual, Mrs. Gordon was in the dining room before him, enthroned behind the coffee urn, engaged on the newspaper. Jim never saw the paper at breakfast, but had snatches of the news read aloud to him. Mrs. Gordon thought it silly to have two morning papers come to the house, so Jim read his at the office.

The dining room of the old Slater house faced the garden. The windows, opened to their widest to let in what there was of morning freshness, were filled with green light that played through the room in ripples, so that the place was like a cave at the bottom of a shallow green lake. Green sparks touched here and there in the room—the top of the coffee urn, a facet or two of the silver service on the heavy walnut sideboard, the glassware and table appointments. In spite of the ugly furniture that had come into the house with the mother of the departed John Slater—a bride of the walnut-and-blue-tile period—the room would have been a very pleasant place in which to drink coffee and eat muffins and bacon, except for the people in it.

"I suppose you couldn't refuse to let them use the office for this business of the sheriff's," Mrs. Gordon greeted her husband.

The remark seemed to require no answer, so he made none, but took his place at the table and unfolded his napkin, relieved by the omission of the customary morning remarks about his usual tardiness.

"I wonder how Miss Marsh will like it—having this

'Captain' Jeffers around."

"It will be only for a day," said Jim Gordon. "She isn't busy. She can use my office if she wants to."

"I didn't mean that. But of course you remember about her affair with Norman Jeffers."

"Why, no. I didn't know they knew each other."

"Of course you know. One of those wartime romances. Engaged just before he went to France. They married the day after he got back and started off on a honeymoon. But next day she was home and they got the marriage annulled. Nobody ever knew just what happened. Norman Jeffers didn't show his face around here for years and when he came back he was just a sort of bum. Mr. Hathaway gave him a job in the garage just out of the goodness of his heart, I guess."

Jim Gordon, sunk as he was in his own misery, had given little thought to Miss Marsh as a person. She was spinsterish and capable and minded her own business.

Mrs. Gordon rattled the paper. "I see Harold Breen came back," she remarked.

"What!" The news hit Jim Gordon like a blow between the eyes. Harold had come back. Milly! Where was Milly?

Mrs. Gordon turned the page. "Poor old Grandma Breen was calling for him. Do you suppose he really killed Will Breen? I don't see why the sheriff didn't put him in jail. The paper says, 'Young Breen was questioned by Sheriff Flagler and was released on his own recognizance.' Whatever that means."

Mrs. Gordon did not happen to glance up or she must have noticed Jim's death-like pallor and the working of his face.

"I never thought anything of Harold Breen, "she went on," but he seems too young and futile to be a murderer. It's a good thing, perhaps, that Milly isn't at home. I sometimes think she hasn't really got over her silly affair with Harold. But I must say I still think it was very strange of her to go off that way to visit Clara without saying anything to me."

Jim Gordon had no heart to repeat the story he had invented to cover Milly's departure—of the friends who had stopped in a car, wanting her to go with them for a little trip—the early hour—the wish not to disturb Mrs. Gordon—He got staggeringly to his feet.

"Going already, Jim? Why, you haven't drunk your coffee. And I do wish you could remember to fold your napkin! It's such a small thing to ask of you, but you never do it. Somebody has to fold it, you know."

Jim folded the napkin, with fingers made clumsy by their trembling. It was the easiest and quickest way to avoid discussion. He muttered something about not feeling hungry and wanting to get to the office early.

He was in the hall. He took his hat from the rack—not consciously, but thanks to a habit reflex. He was in the street. His feet took him along.

Mrs. Paradise saw him go by, and noticed nothing unusual about him. He was, she supposed, on his way to inquire after Grandma Breen's health. He seemed to her an amiable, ordinary person. If she had caught even a passing glimpse of what was going on in him—the storm of fear, anger, and love that raged in him—she would have been frightened out of her wits. Never in her life had she harbored an emotion one-tenth as violent.

Harold was in the driveway beside the house, about to start his car. He looked bathed and brushed, very young and blond. Grave, of course—he was on his way to keep his appointment with the sheriff.

The older man confronted him, haggard, dark, his burning eyes under their shaggy brows like holes burned in a blanket.

"Where's Milly?" His voice was low, but something in

the tone stabbed the boy with fear.

"Isn't she at home?" he stammered. "I left her there—at the garden gate—"

"When?"

"Last evening."

"Did you and Milly have a quarrel?"

"Not—exactly. When she told me about Uncle Will I was angry. She shouldn't have let me go off that way, as though I was running away. See here, Mr. Gordon, you knew about it, too. It wasn't fair."

"I was thinking about Milly," said the man. "I suppose you know why she had to get away."

The color slowly drained out of the boy's face. "Oh, no!" he cried. "Oh, I never guessed—she didn't tell me." He slumped in the seat of the car, all the life gone out of him.

The man's stern face softened. "I see you didn't know," he said. "But Milly's gone. We must find her—if it isn't too late."

"You don't think she would—do something to herself? Listen, Mr. Gordon, she tried to get on a train yesterday when we were coming home. I wouldn't let her. Perhaps—"

Mrs. Paradise came out on the vine-screened porch. "Harold!" she called. "Harold, Sheriff Flagler just called up on the telephone and says for you to go right on down to his office."

"I've got to go, Mr. Gordon," the boy said in an agonized voice. "I'm—as good as under arrest. I suppose you know."

"Don't say a word about this to Sheriff Flagler, or to anybody else. Do you hear me? I'll handle it." The man was terrifying.

"I'll—I'll do just what you say, Mr. Gordon. I—"

"Harold," Mrs. Paradise called again, "you go right along. The sheriff sounded kind of mad."

"I've just got to go!" Harold started the engine and the man stood aside.

"That you, Mr. Gordon?" called Mrs. Paradise from the porch. "I'm right sorry to send Harold off that way when you were talking to him. Won't you come in and see Grandma Breen? She feels lots better this morning."

Her bright, beady eyes peered out from between the vines like the eyes of an alert and curious little animal. What was Jim Gordon talking to Harold about so earnestly, she wondered.

"I'm glad Mrs. Breen is better," the man said quietly. "Please tell her so. Mrs. Gordon will be in to see her later, I'm sure."

He lifted his hat to the inquisitive eyes behind the vines and turned away.

Mrs. Gordon, still sitting at the breakfast table, sipping a second cup of coffee and scanning the "society notes" in the paper, heard him on the stair.

"That you, Jim?" she called. "I thought you'd gone to the office."

"I forgot something," the man mumbled. "Had to come back."

"Your briefcase, I suppose," said Mrs. Gordon, in a tone of patient contempt. "It's a wonder to me you don't forget your shoes or your head." She went back to the paper.

Jim Gordon went direct to his chest of drawers and to the top drawer where his revolver was kept. When he felt its cold hardness under the pile of clean handkerchiefs, he made a queer little choked sound of relief—like a sob. Not that, at any rate.

He opened the door of Milly's room and stood there a long time, looking at the narrow bed under its blue and white spread, at the dressing table with its silly blue flounces and the mirror with the fringe of dance programs, snapshots, cards, and theater stubs stuck in around the rim. A breath of rose-scented air from the garden puffed the light curtains and mingled with the sweet girl-perfumes of the room—lotions, powders, sachet. Tears burned in his eyes like fire. Milly!

"What on earth are you looking for, Jim Gordon?" His wife's exasperated voice came up the stairwell. She must have come out of the dining room into the hall below. "I suppose I'll have to come up and find it for you." He heard her foot on the stair.

"It's all right, Sarah," he called in a choked voice. "I've found it. You needn't come up."

CHAPTER 17

IT WAS HOT, out on the road to Deland. The weeds along the fences were gray with dust, and the sky—even at this hour in the morning—was colorless with heat. Nothing seemed alive except the brave, glittering corn that seemed almost incandescent with joy under the July sun.

The sheriff, with Harold beside him, drove along slowly.

"Watch out close, son, and see if you can find the place," he said.

There was something about the boy, this morning, that the sheriff could not understand—an anguish of fear in his eyes and in his whole bearing. Last night he had felt sure the boy was telling him the truth and that he had had no hand in the taking-off of his uncle. This morning the sheriff did not feel so sure. After all, Harold was the logical suspect—plenty of motive, the opportunity, it all checked.

The sheriff felt very old and weary. He wished there was no such thing as duty to one's oath of office. He did not want to accuse this boy, to put him behind bars, to send him perhaps to the electric chair or at the best to the living death of prison. Each of us has only one life—one little short life. Once blasted it can never be regained. . . .

Harold leaned out of the car, scanning the edge of the road.

"It was right about here—Stop! Here it is, I am almost sure. See that broken weed and those tracks?"

The sheriff drove ahead for a few yards and parked. Together he and the boy walked back to where the broken weed lay black and withered on the sun-baked ground. It showed clearly the marks of a tire across its bruised stem. This was the place.

The sheriff got down heavily on his stiff knees beside the

track and went over the ground, inch by inch. He found the spot where the foot of a jack had stood and stones that had been used to chock the wheels. And there, in the folds of a big, hairy burdock leaf, close to the ground, a splash of something dark. Oil? No. Something else. The sheriff took his penknife from his pocket, cut the stem of the leaf close to the ground and carefully folded the leaf together over the hard, brownish cake it held.

"Find anything, Mr. Flagler?" called the boy.

He was searching at a little distance among the tall white clover and tangle of weeds in the dry ditch.

"Found where he set up the jack," answered the sheriff.

He stood up among the weeds, in his hand the folded leaf. A car came along the road, and the driver, recognizing the sheriff, slowed for a stop, but the sheriff waved to him to go on. Two crows got up heavily from among the corn and flapped away, cawing their hoarse annoyance at being disturbed. Far off somewhere a dog was barking—a tied-up dog, barking in a steady, hopeless way. From horizon to horizon lay the gently rolling fields of that rich land, clothed in the tasseled ranks of corn. Smells of heat and dust and coarse growing things, the constant whine of a million, million tiny insects that rose and fell in slow waves. A splash of dried blood in the folds of a wilting leaf.

The boy cried out suddenly. His foot had struck something hard among the weeds of the ditch. He came running and stumbling back, white and shaking, with the thing in his hand.

The sheriff took the thing. The sun glinted blue from its short barrel.

"Know this gun, son?" he asked in his heavy voice.

"It looks like—I'm almost sure—Uncle Will's gun. He always had one in the car. He sometimes carried a good deal of money, you know, and he was afraid of a holdup."

"Well, we can check that, I guess. Too bad you picked it

up like you did—might have been fingerprints. Maybe still are. We'll find out." The sheriff took out his handkerchief and wrapped the gun carefully. "See if you can find a shell. Ought to be a shell somewhere. If you find it, don't pick it up. Call me."

The sheriff found the shell. It was some distance away, caught against the stem of a tall mullein plant against the fence. The action of the gun could not have thrown it so far. The murderer must have picked it up and thrown it. Well, there it was—a tiny brass cylinder through which death had come to one man and perhaps holding on its surface what would bring the death of another. The sheriff had a momentary impulse to grind the thing into the ground with his heel, but instead he took a piece of paper from his pocket and, picking up the shell with a bit of stick, wrapped it carefully and stowed it away.

The boy was still searching at a little distance. The sheriff called to him and together they drove back to town.

"We'll just take your fingerprints, Harold, while you're here," the sheriff said heavily when they were once more back in his office. "It's like this: The man that shot that gun handled that shell—and he couldn't have wiped it clean after he handled it. If there's fingerprints on it, and yours don't check, that'll let you out, son."

He watched the boy's face for a flicker of fear, but saw none. He got out the ink pad and the printed forms—one for each hand.

"How soon will you—know?"

"Not for two or three days. We got no fingerprint expert here in Keedora. This cartridge and these prints have to go to Chicago to be checked. I guess you've no need to worry."

Again he studied the boy from under his half-closed eyelids.

The boy paled.

"See here, Mr. Flagler," he cried, "you don't think I—"

He choked.

"To tell the truth, Harold, I don't," the sheriff comforted him. "But till this thing is cleared up, everybody that ever had anything to do with Will Breen has got to be considered under suspicion. You just pray there's fingerprints on this shell. And if there's anything you haven't told me, you'd better come clean. There's something on your mind—since last night."

The boy hesitated. He wanted to tell the sheriff about Milly, but he had promised he wouldn't.

"I—there isn't anything I can tell you," he said at last. "It's—I'm bothered about something, but it hasn't anything to do with Uncle Will."

"Your grandma taking this pretty hard?"

"Grandma's all right, I guess. She doesn't know anyone suspects me. If she did, it might kill her. She—her heart, you know."

"Your grandma sets a lot of store by you, Harold."

"Yes. She always sided with me—against Uncle Will when we had—arguments. She—"

"Well, go on home and see what you can do for her, son. Don't go off anywhere for a while."

"You mean—I'm sort of under arrest?"

"Oh, no. But we don't know what'll break, and I want you where I can find you."

"Can I go out tomorrow and help look? This search it said about in the paper?"

"No. You come down here if you want to, though. I'll be right here next to the telephone all day."

A deputy came in to say that two gentlemen from Chicago—from the *Record-Herald*—wanted to talk with the sheriff. Wally Price was with them.

"Damned newspaper pests!" the sheriff muttered. "Oh, all right. Let them in. Go out that other door, Harold. And remember, you stick around home."

CHAPTER 18

THE WHOLE TOWN was in a ferment all that day—Saturday—with preparations for the mass search for a "corpus delicti," announced for Sunday. All day people streamed in and out of the offices of the Keedora Realty Company where Captain Jeffers sat behind Jim Gordon's desk and handed out assignments of territory to captains of squads, while Miss Marsh ran off on the mimeograph sheets of instructions all neatly tabulated, 1, 2, 3, up to 12.

All over town tremendous baking of pies, boiling of eggs, mixing of mayonnaise, squeezing of lemons, icing of cakes were in progress. Small boys ground at the cranks of ice-cream freezers on scores of back porches. The bakeries were all sold out of sandwich buns by noon and had to telephone to neighboring towns for help. Mr. Laubesheimer had not so much as an ounce of butter, a leaf of lettuce, or a can of deviled ham left in stock when at ten o'clock that evening he put on the night-light and locked the door of his shop.

Tourists passing through heard what was in progress and decided to stop over for the excitement and the free lunch promised for the morrow. The campground at the edge of town overflowed into all the neighboring vacant lots, and cots were set up in the sample rooms at the hotel. The soft-drink places had to put on extra "help" and the thirsty stood three deep before the counters clamoring to be served; the New York Store was jammed with people buying sun hats, paper cups, and picnic sets. There was a great run on rubber boots to outfit the Elks who had captured the choice assignment of searching the river. An enterprising dance orchestra was arranging to put on an impromptu dance at Webster's Grove, and the Keedora *Bugle* issued an "extra" for the first time since the Armistice.

It may be supposed that Mr. William Breen, if his aware-ness was still hovering over Keedora, must have been con-siderably amazed by some of the results of his sudden passing; and the killer, too, if not completely occupied by remorse, must have had a feeling of bewilderment. Here was a grim, secret drama working itself out in terms of sandwiches and iced tea, to the inspiring jingle of overfed cash registers and the clack of gasoline pumps.

Meanwhile, Grandma Breen lay on her big bed in a pleasantly darkened room with the nurse hovering about to feel her pulse and bring her cold bouillon, and her beloved Harold sitting beside her holding her hand.

Only Jim Gordon was suffering. He had no idea what to do. There was nothing he could do. He must find Milly—and quickly—but he had no idea where to look. He thought of Milly as he had seen her last in the dark hallway, holding up her pale little face for his farewell kiss, and his pain was so intense that it stopped his breath.

She had a little money—the roll of bills he had filched from his wife to give her. Harold said she had tried to take a train—He went first to the railroad station.

But arrived at the "depot," he found he could not just go up to the station agent and ask, "Did Milly Slater leave on any train last night or today?" If he were to do that, the word of Milly's disappearance would be passed all over town. The station agent was known as Keedora's chief disseminator of news. The thing must be got at obliquely.

The waiting room was almost empty at that hour, be-tween trains. A fat Italian father with a fatter Italian mother and four sticky, besmudged cherubs occupied one corner of the place with their restless persons and assortment of bulging bags and boxes. There was no one else.

The station agent leaned on the shelf in front of the little window in his partition.

"Ticket, Mr. Gordon?"

"No, Chester. I was just wondering how much passenger traffic you are having the last few days."

Surely, if Milly had been a part of that traffic the man would mention it.

"Nobody a-tall going out," said the agent, "but plenty of folks coming in. You'd be surprised. Regular boom. They're running an excursion special down from Des Moines tomorrow morning. What for? Why, for this show the sheriff's putting on."

Jim Gordon had forgotten all about William Breen and the projected corpse-hunt.

"Oh, thank you," he said vaguely.

He turned and went out, followed by the puzzled eyes of the station agent.

"Now, what's biting that guy?" the station agent asked himself. "Acted kind of goofy—kind of not all there. Never heard of Jim Gordon getting drunk."

He considered the matter till train time, but came to no conclusion. Coming back to the problem after the train had come and gone, he decided that Jim Gordon was doing a little undercover work on the Breen case. Checking up to see if a suspect had left town. Something mighty mysterious about that man Gordon, he perceived he had always thought. Might be a Federal agent. Later he passed this theory along, and in this way Jim Gordon acquired a reputation that caused certain fellow-citizens to give him a wide berth for the next few years. He never noticed and never knew.

After leaving the station, he drove about aimlessly for hours—out past the country club where men in plus fours and girls in gay-colored sports clothes were whacking little white balls about in the blazing sun; past Webster's Grove where the dance promoters were busy stringing paper lanterns between the trees; past the slaughterhouse with its bestial stenches; out first one and then another of the dusty highways between the cornfields. He seemed to see Milly's little figure always before him and half expected to come upon her, waiting for him beside the road.

He was many miles deep in the farmland when the idea suddenly came to him that there might be a message from her at the office. Of course there would be a message. She wouldn't just go away like that without leaving some word for him. He whirled about in a cloud of dust and started back for town at the old car's highest speed. On the way he passed the sinister old house with the mansard roof, but no emanation of Milly's need for him reached out from it to stop him. He knew nothing about the place or the illegal art practiced there.

He parked in his usual place, up the side street, and reached his office. He found the place full of people and activity. He was bewildered for a moment till he remembered what was going on. He pushed the people aside blindly, not seeing the odd looks they gave him, and made his way to the table where Miss Marsh was busy with the mimeograph.

"Anyone to see me, Miss Marsh?" he asked. "Any messages?"

He wanted her to say, "Why yes, Mr. Gordon, Miss Slater is waiting for you in the inner office." But she didn't say it. She merely shook her head.

"Nobody telephone?"

He could hardly believe there was no word, he had so firmly convinced himself that there would be a message.

Miss Marsh stopped the machine to answer.

"Mrs. Gordon called up," she said. "She wants you to take home six lamb chops and a quarter's worth of rice when you go. I made a note—it's on your desk."

She turned back to the machine, and white sheets of paper began to flow into it again, to come out neatly blackened "INSTRUCTIONS," 1, 2, 3, 4—up to 12.

Gordon went into his private office and shut the door. He sat down at his desk—bare but for the bit of paper with his wife's message written out in Miss Marsh's neat "library" hand. "Six lamb chops; a quarter's worth of rice." He did nothing—just sat and stared at the blank wall.

After a long time Miss Marsh tapped on the door and came in.

"Captain Jeffers and I are going out to supper now, Mr. Gordon—if there's nothing you want?"

If he had been capable of noticing anything, he would have remarked the unusual note in her voice when she said, "Captain Jeffers and I," and he might have remembered what Mrs. Gordon had told him about Miss Marsh and her wartime romance. Under and over and through the turmoil in the outer office during that exciting day a little private drama had been playing itself to some conclusion that would, perhaps, be reached at supper.

Morning. Miss Marsh waiting—with an unusual spot of color on each cheek—for a step in the hall, a remembered voice. The door opening.

"Is this Mr. Gordon's—? Oh! You. I didn't know. I'll go."

"Why should you go?" Her voice sounded hoarse, unnatural to her. "I'm Mr. Gordon's secretary. He told me to give you what assistance I can."

They stood face to face. She thought with a pang of pity, "How terribly thin and sick he looks! And his eyes—!" A sob rose in her throat, but she choked it back.

He thought: "Why! there are crow's-feet in the corners of her eyes, and her throat isn't round and soft any more. She's not a youngster any more. But she's Flora."

Somehow the fact that she was no longer a girl did not make a stranger of her. This was not the girl he remembered with so much pain, but it was still Flora. He felt a surge of indignation. All this time he had kept out of her way—she had no right to let him in for this.

She held out her hand to him and he took it awkwardly. Her eyes, he saw, were swimming in tears. He wanted to say something to her, but no words came. There was, really, nothing to be said—nothing, that is, that it would be safe or wise or kind to say.

The door opened to admit the first volunteer corpse-hunter, and the situation was saved.

From that moment till the rush thinned out at supper time, there was no chance for words in private, but all day each was aware of the other. Remembering.

No use, the man thought, trying to sidestep the scene that, plainly, she meant to have. Better to get it over with. He'd take her to supper later on and let her say her say. . . .

"Miss Marsh, an instruction sheet, please, for this man."

"There's a button off his shirtsleeve," Miss Marsh was thinking, as she fed paper into the mimeograph machine. "I suppose he'll ask me to go out to supper with him. If he does I'll say no. Kindly, of course. It's very painful, seeing him again. I wish I had stayed away."

But she didn't wish it. Something in her was singing. She found herself composing little speeches like: "You must not blame yourself too much, Norman. I was at fault, too. Perhaps, if I—"

His poor shoes! His poor work-scarred hands!

CHAPTER 19

THE SHRILLING of the telephone at his elbow broke in on Jim Gordon's stupor of misery. At first he did not answer. It would be his wife telling him to come right home to supper. It rang again and again, and finally he took the thing off its hook.

"Mr. Gordon?" The voice was Harold Breen's. "Mr. Gordon—I know where Milly is. She—I can't tell you over the telephone. I'm coming down to your office."

For a moment Jim could not speak.

"Have you finished talking?" came the telephone operator's metallic voice.

"Mr. Gordon—did you hear? I'm coming right down."

"You don't mean?" Jim spoke slowly and thickly. It seemed almost impossible to make his tongue move against his teeth.

"She's—sick. We've got to get right out there—"

When Harold's flivver slid to a stop at the curb a few minutes later, Jim was standing there on the corner, waiting.

"We'd better take your car, Mr. Gordon," Harold said. "It's bigger than mine."

"Tell me—"

"She called. Not Milly—that 'Dr.' Paramene, from that nursing-place out by the country club. She said—she said Milly's pretty sick and to come and get her right away."

It was not far, at the rate the big car was traveling, though it had been far enough to Milly, on foot in the darkness.

It was evening again. Street lights were coming on. They passed a clanging open streetcar full of yellow light and girls in fluttery summer dresses with their attendant swains, joyriding for coolness in the breathless heat. They were on the country road in a cloud of choking dust.

"Turn here—to the left."

Before them was the sinister old house in its untidy thicket.

A hatchet-faced woman in hospital white opened the door. She stood as though to bar the way, and from behind her gushed out a wave of stale air loaded with the smell of drugs.

"I'm Mr. Gordon," Jim said quietly. "Milly Slater's step-father. I've come for Milly."

The woman stood aside to let the two men enter.

"She's pretty bad," said the woman. "You understand, I can't let her stay here."

She led the way up the stair—a stair of pride, sweeping upward in a fine, bold curve of walnut. Instead of a deep-piled velvet carpet, though, it wore a ribbon of black rubber down the center, the edge of each tread shod with metal.

To Harold, in the excited state of his mind, every detail of the place stood out stark and enormous, like things seen in a nightmare. He saw the stained walls, bare of any ornament; the arched window on the landing whose florid stained glass had been mended with a single white pane; the wide upper hallway with its six closed doors. From behind one of the doors came a sobbing moan.

It was not Milly, though, that moaned.

Milly lay on a narrow, high, white bed in a room where there were three other beds. Her face, turned up to the ceiling, was waxy-white. It was drawn into strange lines. To Harold this was not Milly at all—he would not have known her.

"She's conscious," said the woman, "but terrible weak. She had a hemorrhage, you know. Here's her clothes. The nightgown she's got on belongs to me, but you'd better take her the way she is. You can send back the nightgown."

She busied herself gathering together Milly's pathetic little limp dress from the back of a chair, her saucy little hat, her dusty shoes.

The girl's eyelids fluttered open and she looked up into Jim's face as he leaned above her. A little twitching at the corners of her bloodless lips sketched a smile.

"I knew—you'd—come, Jim," she whispered.

The man stooped and, folding the cotton bed-covering around her, picked the girl up in his arms with infinite care and tenderness.

Her head pillowed on his shoulder like that of a sleepy child.

"That bedspread's mine, but I guess you'll have to take it, too. I want it back, you know. Here, take these."

The woman thrust the bundle of Milly's clothes at Harold and went to open the door.

"Will she—live?" whispered Harold.

"She might," the woman answered. "But I couldn't take the chance of having her die on me out here. Get a blood transfusion right away, though—if you can."

They were down the stair and out in the night. The door clicked shut behind them.

"Get in front and drive," Jim directed Harold. He, with Milly in his arms, got into the back of the car." Drive carefully, but don't waste any time."

Harold drove. Each tiny jolt in the road brought his heart to his mouth. He crawled along. Cars came up behind and honked and slid past, enveloping them in dense rolls of dust.

"You can drive faster, now," said Jim Gordon's quiet voice. "She's unconscious."

"Where are you going to take her?"

"Home, of course. Drive to the back gate. Then you walk around to the front of the house and ring the doorbell. Tell Mrs. Gordon that Grandma Breen's been asking for her. Get her out of the house. I want Milly in bed and the doctor here before she gets back. I can't attend to her now."

"Is Milly—?"

"God knows," said the man.

When the car stopped, he got out with Milly in his arms. She was very still. Perhaps she was already dead, but he thought he could feel a faint heartbeat. He let himself into the house by the door on the garden. The back passage was dark except for a faint reflection from the light in the front hall. He could hear his wife's voice and Harold's mumble. "Why, of course, I'll run over, Harold—" And then the bang of the screen door. He made his way to the front of the house and up the stair.

Harold had come back. He must have run all the way, for he was panting.

He called: "Mr. Gordon, what can I do?"

"Call Dr. Jacobson and tell him it's urgent. To come just as quick as he can."

He carried Milly into her room and laid her gently down on the narrow bed. The house was very still—no sound but the anxious throb of his own heart in his ears and the shrilling of night insects outside in the garden. The rising moon shone full in at the window and lay in a blue pool on the bed. Milly seemed floating in it.

The man dropped to his knees beside the bed and pressed his lips to the girl's cold forehead. His whole heart went out to her—to this poor gentle little creature with her broken life and her tortured body. He would gladly have poured into her drained veins every drop of his own blood so that she might live. Why did he want her to live? Why does anyone want to live or to have those he loves go on bearing the anguish of existence? Life is a sorry business. But he could not let Milly die.

When the doctor came and had made his examination, his face grew grim.

"I doubt if she'll pull through, Gordon," he said brutally. "I'll try to save her, of course. But you know what this piece of deviltry may cost me? It's the penitentiary in this State. We'll have to make a transfusion right away. Can't stop to make tests. It's the only chance."

Harold, who had been standing outside in the hall beside the open door, now came in and approached the bed.

"Take my blood, Dr. Jacobson," he begged.

"So, it's you, is it?" said the doctor. "All right. Take off your shirt. Lie down here on the bed beside her. Get me some boiling water, Gordon. Telephone for a nurse. Get Mrs. Parsons. She knows how to keep her mouth shut."

And so began the fight for Milly Slater's life. The doctor and the nurse who presently arrived were too busy to notice the man who sat so still there in the corner of the room. He kept out of the way and asked no questions.

Toward morning the doctor straightened his tired back.

"Well, nurse," he said, "I guess that's about all we can do." He stood looking down at the girl, lying so still and white on the narrow white bed.

"Yes, Doctor."

The nurse rattled bits of steel in a basin of carbolic. She set the doctor's little black bag on a chair and began putting the instruments and little bottles away in their proper places. Outside the birds were beginning to twitter and whistle and flutter among the leaves. A fragrant, damp breath from the garden stole in through the open window to mingle with the strong drug odors. The cool light of dawn began to yellow the light of the room.

So it was all over. Jim Gordon got to his feet and came close to the bed. Milly's eyes were closed, the long dark lashes startling against the waxy-whiteness of her softly rounded cheeks. "I can't bear it," thought the man, but he stood there quietly enough, though his heart was breaking.

"Great thing, youth," said the doctor, rolling down his sleeves and buttoning the cuffs. "Shock like that to an older person and, poof! she's gone. Milly here'll be as right as a trivet in a few weeks."

"Then—she isn't—?"

"Dead? Good Lord, no. Put a cot or a couch or something in here, will you, so the nurse can get a little rest. I'll be in again about noon."

The doctor picked up his rusty black bag, a veteran of many life-and-death battles, and went his way.

Jim went out into the garden. The sudden relief after his hours of agony had left him in an odd condition of emotional suspension. It seemed to him that he did not feel at all. But his senses were all stimulated so that the world appeared to him all new, as though just created, and unbelievably strange and beautiful. He heard every smallest sound, every bird-note, every whisper of the air. He saw every leaf and flower, every blade of sharp green grass, every shade of color in the opalescent sky, every tiny crawling or flying insect. He felt the soft push of the breeze against his face, against his eyeballs. And the beauty of these things was so poignant that it choked him.

It is so that painters, poets, and madmen are privileged to see the world.

CHAPTER 20

NORMAN JEFFERS, waiting for Miss Marsh to put on her hat, wished he had not asked her to have supper with him. The next hour would not, he thought, prove very pleasant for either of them. But he could see she was all tuned up to a scene of reminiscences and regrets. He supposed she would have to have it or she would never let him alone again. Might as well get it over with. Unpleasant but necessary, now they had met. He added that undesired meeting to the reckoning against William Breen that he carried in a secret and bitter place in his heart. Why, the man was poisonous even when dead—if he was dead.

Miss Marsh, fussing with herself before the mirror of the washroom, felt twittery, and wondered if it might not have been wiser not to accept the invitation to supper. At the restaurant someone who knew their story would be sure to notice them, together after all these years, and there would be talk. But of course she could not get out of it now without hurting his feelings. People would see in their chance association the revival of an old romance. Perhaps that is what she saw in it herself. It is indiscreet to inquire just how far her imaginings were taking her.

"I have an old wreck that was once an automobile," the man said, as they went together down the stair to the street. "It runs, after a fashion. If you aren't too proud, perhaps we might ride around a while and cool off. That office of yours is beastly hot, if you don't mind my saying so."

"A little ride would be very pleasant," said Miss Marsh primly.

"Out to the Spring? Or would you rather go in some other direction?"

"The road to the Spring is the prettiest, I think."

The "wreck" was really a wreck—an ancient roadster without a top and with most of the body missing. When she saw it she had qualms, but climbed in without hesitation, hiding her dismay.

"I have an idea !" she said. "Why don't we stop at the Pink Butterfly tearoom and get one of those picnic boxes Mrs. Boyle puts up, and eat our supper at the Spring?"

He looked at her sharply. "Ashamed to be seen with me in public, Flora?" he asked, in a tone amused rather than resentful. "Well, you're right, at that."

"Norman! Of course not—! How can you say such a thing!" She was close to tears already.

"I only said you were perfectly right. Where is this 'Pink Butterfly' place? I haven't been infesting tea shops lately to any great extent."

He parked his disreputable car in front of the tearoom and went in. Miss Marsh remained in the car. The sensible thing to do, of course, would be simply to get out of the car and go home, but her getting-out muscles refused to respond to the suggestion, and she was still there, perched up on the skeleton seat, when the man came out of the shop with a square paper box under his arm.

"I win," he said. "I made a bet with myself that you would stick it out."

Very few words were exchanged on the drive to the Spring. Both were thinking of other evenings in younger summers. The same road; the same wafts of fragrance from the roadside tangle of wild roses; the same corn standing tall and strong in the heat; the same companion. But all with what a difference!

The sun shone level across the fields into their eyes. It was a huge red balloon standing on the rim of the world. Then it was half a balloon; and then it was gone. The sky melted from gold to green, to blue. Slowly the soft twilight gathered.

They both spoke, at the same moment and in the same words.

"It's been a long time—"

"It's been a long time—"

"I was going to say," Miss Marsh started again in the resulting silence, "that it's been such a long time, Norman. We can be friends now, can't we?" She was a little breathless with emotion.

"You think that would be 'pleasant'? No, Flora, you and I can't be friends."

She made a little "Oh—!" of pain.

"I don't mean," he went on, "that I haven't forgiven you. I have. Long ago. I mean it. You were perfectly right in what you did. I am as worthless, as hopeless, as you pointed out to me. I didn't believe it then, of course, but the proof is not far to seek."

"*You* have forgiven *me!*"

"Of course. But it would be silly to think of being 'friends.' Even this meeting is a mistake, and I see you realize that as well as I. But of course in a way it's 'pleasant.' "

"Please turn around and take me back, Norman," Miss Marsh said in a choked voice. "You are—unkind."

"We're here now," he pointed out reasonably. "Might as well eat supper the way we planned. It will save time. There's still plenty of work to be done at the office tonight, you know."

He brought the car to a stop in the open space under the trees used as a parking place by visitors to the Spring.

"Someone here before us," he remarked, noting that another car already stood there. "Well, we won't bother them if they don't bother us."

They both remembered later that the car had stood there, but neither ever spoke of having seen it. They were too much preoccupied with their own affairs to have any thought of William Breen and the missing black sedan.

It was a pleasant place, much beloved by children who came in the springtime to pick the nodding red and yellow columbines and waxy bloodroot and dainty wild pansies, or to search for the elusive "walking fern" for high-school herbaria. A spot infested at times by Sunday-school picnics, and frequented by lovers in the sweet summer evenings. It was a little glen hollowed out of the shelving limestone, hemmed in by white cliffs—full of tall old trees, green grasses, and the music of the famous spring that gushed, cold and sweet, out of the rock wall; unfailing in even the hottest, driest summer. There was even a cave, clammy and dark, where a legendary catamount had once laired.

The place held memories for them both. It had been a mistake to come here.

The man got out of the car and walked over to the spring. The same old tin cup hung there from the same bit of dead branch. He dipped a cupful of the clear water and drank. He stood there for a long time. Something was happening in him. Something he didn't want to have happen.

The woman sat in the car, too angry and hurt and miserable to move.

He filled the cup and brought it to her, dripping, but she would not take it from him. He poured the water out on the grass and returned the cup to its peg. He got the paper box out of the car, set it on the running board, seated himself beside it with his back to the woman, and began to eat.

"I'm behaving like a pettish child," poor Miss Flora told herself. "How can I stop behaving this way?"

She knew that the situation was ridiculous, but she had never felt less like laughing. She wanted to cry. She was going to cry—she couldn't help it. She bowed her face in her hands and sobs shook her thin shoulders.

"Flora, you little fool!" The man's voice was rough with

unwilling tenderness and a hint of laughter. "Come out of it! There's fried chicken and fruit salad, and a thermos of coffee—"

She turned toward him her face bleary with tears. He was standing, now, looking down at her with the expression she remembered so well.

"If you'd—get me a cup of water from the spring—"

He stooped quickly and kissed her full on the lips. Till that moment he had not touched her. He went off, whistling, through the green half-light to the spring. When he came back with the brimming cup she was seated on the running board of the car with a paper napkin from the box spread tidily across her blue linen knees.

"We haven't changed much, have we, Norman?" she said timidly.

The words were unfortunate. His expression was all at once bleak and hard. He turned away and stood leaning against a tree with his back to her.

"Changed!" he said. "My—God!"

"Norman, what's the matter? Norman! I don't understand."

She went to him and tried to put her arms around him, but he pushed her away—gently enough, but firmly.

"Come along," he said. "Let's go back."

They drove back in silence. It was not yet fully dark, for the picnic at the Spring had taken but a very short time. The man drove fast and the warm air rushed past like a soft hurricane. Miss Marsh felt—in spite of the abrupt finish of their scene in the glen—an old happiness in the purple twilight and the nearness of this man. She felt again his lips on hers. In all these years no one had kissed her. She held her hat in her lap and let the wind do what it liked with her hair.

But—"Oh!" she said suddenly as the lights of the town twinkled ahead at a turn in the road. "The thermos bottle!

Mrs. Boyle will want it back. We forgot it."

"I wouldn't go back after the crown jewels of Russia," the man said gruffly. "Don't worry. I paid a deposit on the thing. Your Mrs. Boyle won't be out a cent."

"Oh—but—"

"I'm taking you home," he said. "Where do you live?"

"I'm going back to the office with you, Norman, to finish—"

"No. You're not. I can do anything that has to be done."

Meekly she named her street and number.

But when the car stopped before the modest house in which she had her tiny suite of "housekeeping rooms," she did not at once alight.

"Norman," she said with a rush. "This isn't good-bye. I want you to come to see me. Tomorrow."

"Forget it, Flora," he muttered. "I'm never going to see you again. Get that straight. I mean it."

"But—you kissed me. I don't understand—"

"You don't have to understand, thank God. Why, Flora, if you guessed what I've done, what I've become, you'd scream and run from me. I should have cleared out right away—this morning when I found you in that office."

"You don't mean—? That you've committed a—crime?"

"Call it that if you like. But don't be getting any wild idea of reforming me. What's done is done."

His tone was dull and cold. He was in an agony that the woman beside him could not have imagined. Every nerve in his body screamed with pain, and he gripped the wheel to hide the shaking of his hands.

Those who passed along the street, if they noticed at all the two people sitting at the curb in the old car, saw a spinsterish woman with untidy, windblown hair who appeared not to be finding very amusing the shabby, middle-aged, sick-looking man beside her.

"You'll be needing the key to the office," said Miss Marsh at last in a stifled voice. She fumbled in her handbag and produced the key. She got out of the car and stood a moment hesitating. What could she say to him? She sensed finality. "Good-bye, Norman."

He did not trust himself to look at her or to speak. He meshed the gears and the old car moved slowly away.

CHAPTER 21

SUNDAY MORNING BREAKFAST—usually a late and leisurely function with waffles and maple-syrup trimming—was early and hurried on the morning of the great Keedora corpse-hunt.

Mr. Henry Smith gulped his last swallow of coffee, buckled on his shoulder-holster, weighted by his old six-shooter, and slipped a box of cartridges into his pocket.

"It gives me the shivers," said Mrs. Smith, "to see you with that gun."

"Don't worry. I'm not intending to shoot or get shot. But the sheriff said for everybody that's leader of a squad to go armed. We leaders are all made deputy sheriffs for the day, you know."

He felt a bit important, and it showed in his voice.

"You'll be careful?"

"Of course I will." He laughed indulgently. "And you be at the grove by noon, with plenty of lunch, or there'll be trouble in the Smith family. I got to take the car; you can get there on the bus, all right."

"I'm going with the minister and his family. You know there's to be church service. I hope you can get back for that."

"Maybe I can. Depends on how long it takes to cover our sector. But anyhow I'll see you at noon."

He kissed his wife and baby a hasty good-bye and drove away.

All seven members of the Smith squad turned up on time at the appointed meeting place—Webster's Grove. They foregathered about the end of one of the long picnic tables of shiny new yellow boards set up in a great hurry the day before.

"It's like this, fellows," Smith explained to the six earnest faces turned toward him. "We're to take this piece of land south of the river here, from the Larkin road west"—he spread on the table a tracing from the map in Jim Gordon's office. "We're to go over it with a fine-tooth comb. Here, I'll read the instructions." He brought from his pocket a sheaf of papers and spread out before him a mimeographed sheet headed "INSTRUCTIONS."

"You are to search for the following:

(1) The person, dead or alive, of William Breen. Description: height, five feet eleven inches; weight, a hundred and sixty pounds; age, fifty-one; complexion, sallow; eyes, greenish brown, set close together; nose, thin and long; mouth, small and pursy—"

"What does 'mouth pursy' mean?" asked one of the listening group.

"You know—the way Will Breen always held his mouth, like he was thinking about whistling. But never mind the description. I guess we here all knew Will Breen by sight. What clothes, though, was he wearing?"

"Let's see—'suit of lightweight gray worsted, blue silk necktie, white Panama hat, blue silk socks, black shoes. Signet ring on left hand. Open-faced Howard watch on chain, wallet containing letters and small amount of money.' And we are to search for:

(2) Buick sedan, 1932 model, painted black. Motor-meter radiator cap; two spare wheels; license number 69-8745; engine number 17765493.

(3) The person or persons responsible for the disappearance of William Breen and any material evidence, such as bloodstained clothes, implements, etc., etc.

In making this search go over every foot of the ground to make sure the soil has not been disturbed. If places are found where the soil appears to have been disturbed recently, dig until convinced that no evidence will be found.

Search all houses, barns, and buildings, giving particular attention to abandoned houses, old wells, old root cellars and house foundations.

If people living on the property to be searched are unwilling to cooperate, serve on them one of the John Doe warrants with which you have been provided. In case of serious opposition remain on the ground, but take no action without first getting in touch by telephone with the sheriff's office.

No arms are to be carried except by squad leaders, who have been deputized for this emergency and who will go armed. The squad leader will direct the operations in his sector and will be responsible for the diligent prosecution of the search. Reports should be made to the office of the sheriff."

"Well, boys, that's the lay-out."

"Say, there's an old limekiln on the Swatcher place,"said one of the squad. "Spooky kind of place. I'll bet you—"

"We've got to do this job systematically," said Smith. "We can't just poke around in the likely places. We'll start here right along the Larkin road."

"That's Old Man Larkin's big cornfield," said one of the searchers with a sigh. He began already to look somewhat weary and wilted. "A job that's going to be!"

"Well, what did you think this was—a picnic?"

Of course that was exactly what most of the searchers were expecting—a picnic. The thing had picnic aspects; and camp-meeting aspects, when the Methodists began to pray and sing hymns under the trees at the grove. And it had aspects of comedy, melodrama, romance, even of tragedy; but for the most part it turned out to consist of weary miles of walking in the heat, up and down between the proud rows of the corn. "It" might be anywhere.

Old Man Larkin and his hired men and his tall sons came out to help in the search of the great cornfield. The pretty daughter of the house came, too. She laughed a great deal and played with the strings of her pink gingham sunbonnet. She did not wear a sunbonnet because she had no hats. Papa Larkin was a substantial farmer and his daughter had been away to boarding school and college and had many city hats and city clothes. But no doubt she realized just what a pink gingham sunbonnet will do for laughing eyes and a dimpled chin. She was accompanied by a highly decorative collie who followed at her heels with a manner of amiable boredom.

The cornfield yielded nothing of interest to anyone except to the pretty Larkin daughter and to young Fielding—the beau of the squad of searchers. Poor Will Breen, lying in his secret grave "somewhere in Iowa," was the Cupid of this occasion—a meeting that through its results may affect the history of the world. Who can tell?

The hot and disillusioned searchers gathered on the Larkin porch and were refreshed with ice-cold lemonade and sugar cookies. Several began to think up reasons for an immediate return to Keedora.

"Say, fellows," Mr. Smith addressed his squad, "it seems to me we are making too big a job of this thing. If Will Breen was murdered, it happened in the middle of the day, and if he was buried, it must have been somewhere near the road. A man wouldn't carry a corpse a long way from the road, in daylight, to find a place to dig a grave. How far would you say?"

There were various estimates, from ten yards to a hundred.

"Tell you what we'll do—we'll follow the roads, anywhere a car could go, and look for a hundred and fifty yards on each side. How's that?"

The idea met with approval.

"How about that old limekiln?" asked the persistent individual who had mentioned this place before.

An odd look passed between Old Man Larkin and his sons.

"You wouldn't hardly be likely to find anything up there," he said.

"There's a road in, I suppose," said Squad-leader Smith.

"Well, hardly what you'd call a road. Guess there hasn't been a car up there, anyway, for ten years. An old fellow lives up there, too. If anybody's been there he'd have seen them."

Larkin's tone showed a curious reluctance and Smith eyed him sharply.

"If it's a still you're worried about," he said, "forget it. We aren't looking for stills; all we're looking for is a black automobile and maybe a corpse."

At the mention of a corpse the Larkin daughter said "Oh!" and shivered prettily. She and young Fielding had, as a matter of course, taken the hammock at the end of the porch.

Old Man Larkin laughed, and the strained expression vanished from his broad face.

"Well, in that case everything is fine," he said. "You, Tony, go on up and tell old Jimson it's all right. He can put the shotgun away."

One of the sons got up from the porch steps and strolled off.

"Old Jimson," Larkin went on, "heard about the search over the radio and he came down here yesterday afternoon all het up and wanted us to turn out and move his outfit for him. I told him it wouldn't be any use—that you'd be sure to find it no matter where he put it. He went away talking to himself and I was kind of afraid he mightn't act too sociable. He makes right good stuff, and repeal hasn't hurt his business any as far as I can see."

"Well, we'll go up and talk to him," said Smith. "I guess we're all rested up. Come along, boys."

The squad got to its various feet—all but young Fielding, who was too well occupied to notice that the work of the day had been resumed. With Larkin to guide them, the squad straggled off across an orchard, through a gate and over a stretch of pastureland to a patch of timber in a hollow. As they came into the hollow they struck a rough road, overgrown with weeds and grass, but still traceable.

As they came into the road, Old Larkin uttered an exclamation: "Well, I'll be!" and they all stopped and looked where he pointed. Clearly to be seen in a bit of damp earth were the impressions of automobile tires.

"Somebody's been along here with a car, all right," said Smith. "Spread out, you fellows, about ten feet apart each side of this road. Take it slow and look close. I'm going on up and see what the old moonshiner has to say."

He and Larkin hurried on up the road while the squad spread out and began slowly beating the brush.

The old limekiln looked like an ideal setting for almost any sort of crime. An outcrop of limestone served as a backdrop. It had been hollowed out by blasting into a bowl-shaped bay. A long time ago, for young trees had rooted in the heaps of waste, and ferns and moss clung against the face of the cliff wherever there was a cranny. In the lip of the bay stood the ruined buildings of the kiln—a squat, wide chimney, arched openings into broken masonry, like the mouths of caverns.

Young Tony Larkin stood at the kiln with a grotesque Rip Van Winkle of an oldster beside him. The old man's manner was exceedingly doubtful; he seemed poised for an instant scuttling away among the rocks, like an old woodchuck.

"It's all right, Jimson," Mr. Larkin reassured him. "This is Mr. Smith from up in Keedora. He's looking for a black automobile, and maybe a dead man. How about it? Know anything? Somebody's been up here with a car, all right."

"It's funny about that car," the old man whined in a high falsetto that issued oddly from his bearded lips. "Two or three days ago, it was. I hearn it when it turned in off the highway. Thought it was Joe. I told Joe never to come up here in that truck of his—don't want no tracks—but Joe, he don't like to walk and sometimes he's in kind of a hurry. I come on out here to give Joe a good bawling-out, but after a while I seen this here car down between the trees in that gap"—he pointed off toward the thicket. "I couldn't see it right good, but I could see it warn't Joe's truck. I ran back in and got me my gun. 'Federals,' I thought. Maybe just some fool picnicker. When I come out, the car was stopped down there by that rock. Couldn't get no closer. A man had the door open and was starting to get out when I yelled. He just got right on back in and turned himself 'round and went away."

The men looked at each other. Here might be the answer to the mystery of William Breen's disappearance.

"What kind of a car, Mr. Jimson?" asked Smith.

"Sort of an ordinary big closed car."

"Black?"

"Might 'a' been. Dark-colored like, anyhow. Couldn't see it too good down among those bushes."

"I suppose you didn't get the numbers on the license plate?"

The old man squinted up his face, apparently in a concentrated effort of memory.

"Weren't no license plate onto it," he said finally.

"How about the man? Would you know him again if you was to see him?"

"How could I? Didn't see nothing but one foot and a hand."

"It looks to me," said Smith, "as though the—murderer—remembered this place and thought it would be a good spot to leave what was left of Will Breen. Not knowing about Jimson's being up here. Jimson scared him off. But of course he might have stopped down there in the gully somewhere—"

"No, sir," said old Jimson decidedly. "He didn't stop nowheres. Noise comes right up the gully like in a tunnel. I heard him the minute he turned in off the highway—he kept right on coming till he got here. And after he turned 'round he kept right on going till he got back on the highway."

"Well, that's that," said Smith, after a pause.

"We'll have to look around through your place here, Jimson, but we won't bother you any."

He hallooed to call his squad together. Old Jimson showed them his still with a good deal of honest pride and insisted that they all sample his distillate. Some of the squad were inclined to linger, but Smith got them away as promptly as he was able. He wanted to report what he had discovered to the sheriff, and it was noon, besides, and time to go back to the grove for the famous picnic lunch that the Ladies' Aid had been busy preparing.

CHAPTER 22

MOST OF THE squads of searchers had a very hot, dull time, with nothing to show for their effort except rubbed heels, scratches and abrasions, clothes torn by barbed wire, faces and necks badly burned by the sun, and a firm conviction that—as an old song declares—"The policeman's lot is not a happy one."

One of the most exciting incidents had to do with a nest of wasps in an old barn on a deserted farm; but though spirited enough, and painful in result, the action had no result as far as the finding of Will Breen's body was concerned.

More serious was the incident of the old well. One Chester Dawes volunteered to explore it at the end of a rope. Though dry, it proved to be full of deadly gases, and Chester was withdrawn in a seriously damaged condition. He was rushed to the first-aid station at the Spring and lived to tell the tale. But he hadn't found Will Breen at the bottom of the well.

A painfully cut foot, sustained by a wading Elk in the river, proved more to the point. It was not a broken bottle on which he had stepped, but the sharp edge of a metal plate—an automobile license plate, identified as one of the pair issued to William Breen for a Buick sedan. The plate was found not far from the spot where the rusty spade had been taken from the river.

The scouring action of the sand had removed any possible fingerprints, so the finding of the plate had little result except to make it more probable that the spade had indeed been used by the murderer.

A squad of Oddfellows, searching the bit of woodland near the head of Arrowhead Creek, thought for a time they had something. They had—though not exactly what they were looking for. Coming over a little hill through the brush, they were surprised to discover a new and apparently occupied cabin where no house was supposed to be. The door was shut and curtains at the windows were drawn, but a pale blue feather of smoke floated above the stovepipe chimney, and a canvas swing-hammock was still swaying as though hastily abandoned.

The leading Oddfellow stepped up on the porch and set his knuckles to the closed door. Nothing happened. He knocked again with the same lack of result.

"Somebody's in there," said one of the supporting Oddfellows. "Suppose Breen was kidnaped and they're holding him—"

"Might be that, all right," said the leading Oddfellow. He drew his revolver from the holster. "The rest of you fellows go back," he directed. "Behind trees, or lie flat. They might come out shooting." His heart knocked against his ribs, and he felt like quite a bit of a hero as he knocked again. "Open this door," he shouted. "We're the law. Got a search warrant."

There was a slight commotion audible and the door was opened—by a young man in shirtsleeves, hair tousled, an old pipe between his teeth.

"What's the idea?" said the young man. And "What's the idea?" said the leading Oddfellow, together.

"Why," said a supporting Oddfellow, emerging from behind his tree, "it's Marshall—principal of the high school."

The rest of the Oddfellows emerged into the open and stood about. The young man held the door and made no motion toward inviting his visitors inside.

"Why didn't you open up when I knocked?" asked the leading Oddfellow truculently. His bluster was the kickback of his strained nerves.

"Asleep. Didn't hear you, I guess," said the young man. "If you'd just as lief put up that gun, I'd feel happier, you know. What's it all about, anyway?"

"Haven't you heard?—about the search?"

"Not a thing. Radio isn't working—battery run down. I take it you weren't looking for me?"

"Seen anything of a black Buick sedan?"

"Not likely! My old flivver is the only thing on four wheels that ever got up that trail. Whose black Buick sedan, if one may inquire?"

His tone was insolent and his manner not in the least friendly.

"Will Breen's. He's disappeared—been kidnaped or murdered, the sheriff thinks."

The look of relief that came over the schoolteacher's face seemed a bit peculiar. His manner became at once more agreeable. He came out on the porch, closing the door behind him.

"I came out here a week ago," he confided. "After being shut up for nine months with three hundred youngsters, it's a relief to get off here by myself. I'm—trying to do a little writing. You see how it is."

He leaned against the closed door and puffed at his pipe. Good-looking young fellow, twenty-eightish, nice blue eyes, athletic shoulders, slim waist. But his feet were not small enough for the slipper that lay on the floor of the porch under the hammock.

One of the Oddfellows recognized that slipper. He kept his eyes turned away from it, though the consciousness of it filled him. It was he who had named the young man.

"Well, if you've been here a week, and haven't seen or heard anything out of the way, I guess we don't need to search around here any more," said the leading Oddfellow. "Come along, guys. It's most noon. We'll go back to the cars and head for that luncheon at the grove. Want to come along, Marshall? Free spread for everybody down at the grove."

But Marshall was not interested in the free spread. He stood on the porch and watched his callers out of sight along the rough track that led back to the main road.

One of the Oddfellows felt very queer. He was a middle-aged Oddfellow who had been "batching" for a week while his pretty wife was away on a visit to her family in Oshkosh. He felt—well, why not admit it? He and Marjorie hadn't been hitting it off too well. It had been agreeable to have the house to himself, to come home to silence, and things left where he had put them. He supposed that he should have done something. He could go back, now, and make a scene. He felt a great reluctance to do anything of the kind, so he went right on walking down the road on the way to lunch at the grove.

There was, though he did not admit it even to himself, a song in his heart. Free! He would get the shabby old leather chair down from the attic and put it where it used to be, with its back half turned toward the reading lamp on the table, and all those silly silk pillows on the couch that kept a man from making himself comfortable with his feet up—he'd make a bonfire in the back yard and burn them up. And the bathroom would not stink of perfume any more—

So presently a lawyer in Reno would have William Breen to thank for his latest fee, and thanks to William Breen another ill-assorted human combination would return to its elements. The Keedora school board would accept with regret the resignation of the brilliant young principal of the high school. This resignation would give Miss Ida Pettibone, sister-in-law of one of the trustees, her chance at the position she had long coveted, and the future of three hundred young people of Keedora would be affected—for good or ill—by the change.

Along this line alone the incalculable effects of William Breen's disappearance would go echoing down the ages.

And there was the leading Oddfellow—he felt a new confidence in himself. He had often wondered whether, at a pinch, he would prove himself hero or craven. He knew, now. The manner in which he had advanced on the mysterious cabin, that might, for all he knew, have housed a gang of desperate criminals filled him with honest pride. The fact that he had flushed only a schoolmaster with an English pipe didn't, after all, make any difference. The thing was to lead directly to his death a few years later—on his refusal to elevate his hands at the order of a person in a black mask. Because of his victim's courageous attack, the black mask would be captured and after the usual costly pomp of court proceedings would "sit on the hot seat," and in this round-about fashion someone would pay the ultimate legal penalty for the murder of William Breen.

"Did you get on to the slipper?" one of the attendant Oddfellows snickered to his companion. "Oh you love-nest! Wonder who she was?"

CHAPTER 23

KEEDORA WAS AS emptied of its folk that Sunday morning as the little town on Keats's Grecian urn.

A few people, though, remained. The sheriff sat in his hot little office under the electric fan with his vest unbuttoned and his feet on his desk and the telephone at his elbow. He was glad not to be out in the sun. He was, he was realizing, beginning to feel his age. Jeffers was out there in the sun, running around and keeping things moving. Good man, Jeffers. Something a little queer about him, of course. Something a little queer about lots of those ex-service guys. Make a good deputy, though. Not much of a job, being deputy sheriff, but better than washing cars. It could be fixed. Old Waldie wanted to quit, anyhow. Waldie could get a watchman's job—Good gosh, but it was hot! The sheriff mopped his face and his thick, red neck.

Where was that Breen Boy? He was to show up this morning. The sheriff picked up the telephone and called the Breen house. It was Mrs. Paradise, still on the job, who answered him. She would call Harold. Harold was lying down—he didn't feel so good. Sick? Well, not exactly. Milly Slater was sick. The doctor thought she was going to die in the night. There'd been a blood transfusion, with Harold the donor. Made him feel kind of limp. Milly? She might live, now, the doctor said. The doctor'd just been in to see Grandma Breen and had brought the news. Grandma was resting comfortable. Was there any news? Had they found—him—yet? She'd go call Harold right away.

"Never mind," said the sheriff in his gentle growl. "Let the kid take it easy."

He hung up and slumped back in his chair. A bluebottle fly buzzed against the window and the electric fan whirred.

The sheriff's eyes closed. He'd lost a lot of sleep these last few nights. He began to make it up. . . .

Jim Gordon ran his old car out of the garage and set out on a long, aimless drive through the country, carrying his cloud of glory with him. It seemed to him that he had never before really seen in their stiff beauty the tall mullein stalks standing in groups about some close-cropped pasture. The whorl of gray-furred leaves flat against the ground, the proud, straight height of them and their spike of lemon-yellow flowers; the faint, hot scent of them. A row of cottonwood trees beside the road with their sparkling leaves dancing in the light air were so beautiful that they turned him faint. A splash of magenta fireweed in a thicket was like a trumpet call.

A measure of sanity returned to him at last, and he was on his way back to town when he was stopped by a dusty wayfarer. It was a stray member of one of the searching squads who had had enough of walking about in the sizzling cornfields. He volunteered the information that as far as he knew nothing had been seen of Will Breen's corpse or the missing sedan. Till that moment Jim had not remembered the famous corpse-hunt or given a thought to William Breen with his greenish eyes, and tight-lipped mouth, his dark blue necktie and his polished shoes, lying peacefully under the sod in his hidden grave.

The discouraged searcher was inclined to be silent and Jim did not question him, but dropped him on Main Street in front of a "beer " sign and went on to his office. He did not feel like going home.

He was surprised to find Miss Marsh sitting with her head on her desk and crying into a damp handkerchief. She must have been crying for a long time—she was all blurry and half dissolved. Jim had never before seen her cry.

He put a kindly hand on her sobbing shoulder—the

whole woman was a-sob—and said, "Tell me the trouble, Flora. Perhaps I can help."

He had never called her anything but "Miss Marsh" before in all the years she had been his secretary.

"It's—about Norman Jeffers," she said. "A long time ago he was—I was—"

"I know about that."

"I hadn't seen him for years, till yesterday. Oh! Mr. Gordon, he behaved so queerly and said such strange things! I'm frightened." She had got herself together a bit, though tears were still overflowing her reddened eyes and sobs still shook her. "I've got to tell somebody. He looks so sick, and his hands—twitch. And he said—he said—he'd committed a crime."

"A crime? What crime?"

She shook her head.

"I don't know. He didn't tell me. But he hated Mr. Breen for something that happened a long time ago. He—"

"And you think—? You're afraid, perhaps, that it was he who killed Will Breen? Is that it?"

She nodded miserably.

"I suppose I ought to tell the sheriff, but I—can't." Her eyes were full of horror. "You see—I love Norman. What I did to him was all wrong. I failed him—long ago, when we were young. I couldn't send him to prison even if—"

"Listen, Flora," said Jim Gordon. "Whatever Norman Jeffers may have done, he didn't murder William Breen."

Something in the conviction of his tone made her look up sharply with a momentary, wild suspicion. He was looking down at her gravely, with the expression of gentle kindliness so characteristic of him.

"He's good!" she thought. "He's probably the best and kindest man in the world."

She reached for his hand and held it against her tear-wet face. "Oh, thank you!" she murmured.

Jim disengaged his hand quietly.

"We'd better go and find Jeffers," he said. "Put on your hat. Any idea where he'd be?"

"He'll be cruising around everywhere," she said. "But he'll come to the Spring sometime, I'm sure—"

"All right; we'll go to the Spring."

Her face, as she saw it in the dressing room mirror, was lamentable—all swollen with crying, and her nose and eyes red as fire. She did what she could with cold water and face powder, but the result was not very satisfactory. The air would help, perhaps. She had been so miserable a few minutes earlier and now she felt full of happiness and courage. Mr. Gordon had done that for her. He was a kind of saint; he would find Norman for her and everything would be all right.

CHAPTER 24

THE GREAT SEARCH began to drag. Squad leaders found it impossible to get all their men together again after the picnic dinner under the trees. Young fellows and their girls strolled away; the older men, feeling very well filled and extremely comfortable, didn't care much about going out again into the sun. Shucks! Looking for a needle in a haystack would be no job at all compared with looking for what was left of Will Breen in all that sea of green. He might be anywhere. The automobile? That might be two thousand miles away by this time.

Other picnickers had left behind an iron spike and a bunch of horseshoes. Several men drifted off shamefacedly in that direction, and presently forgot all about Will Breen or the purpose of the gathering. Mrs. Forsythe happened to mention that she always carried a bridge set in the pocket of her car. Mrs. Eberle had a folding table and Mrs. Evans and Mrs. Hart had folding chairs.

They sought out a secluded spot—in deference to the Sabbath as much as to Will Breen.

"Some people are so fussy about Sunday—we wouldn't want to hurt anybody's feelings."

They agreed, with the first deal, that it didn't seem exactly right—with poor Will Breen—After that other matters absorbed them.

A few conscientious souls, to be sure, set out in the afternoon heat to finish their assignments. The squad captained by Mr. Smith, somewhat reduced in numbers, but encouraged by their adventure of the morning, returned to the task.

But after half an hour or so one of them stopped in his tracks, halfway up a row of corn. "Oh, hell!" he remarked to the glare and the waving tassels high above his head. He turned and went back the way he had come and got into his car.

There was no debate. The others followed his example, and all were soon on their way back to the Spring. The famous corpse-hunt was practically over.

But the great sensation of the day was still to come.

Wally Price had had a discouraging day, and was beginning to realize that the Keedora sensation was a flop. He had coursed about in his car over the entire terrain, but without result except a headache from the sun, a lungful of dust, and a big bill for gas. He had watched the splashing Elks, but missed the sensational find of the license plates. He had seen scores of perspiring citizens hunting up and down between the interminable rows of corn, but arrived too late to see the unconscious man rescued from the well. Now on his dogged rounds he drove in at Webster's Grove.

Matter, the newspaper ace from Kansas City, was there. He had been there all day taking things very easy indeed. He sat in the grass, his back propped against an old tree trunk, talking to a girl—to Wally's girl!

"Hello, feller," he called gaily. "Heard about the big excitement?"

"What? What's happened?"

"Calm yourself! Calm yourself! They haven't found Old Breen as far as I know. Nothing like that. We've been having a baby here at the first-aid station. Fact. If it'd been a boy, I suppose it would have gone through life as William Breen Goggin, but it's a girl. Pearl Goggin. Got her picture. With a start like that and the swell publicity, I suppose she's halfway to Hollywood."

"Oh—shucks!" said Wally, dropping in the grass.

"It was one of those tourists," said Tina. "Poor thing. A lackadaisical husband and three youngsters in a rattletrap flivver. I don't see why people act the way they do."

"And another sensation," Matter went on. "A brave outfit find what they take for a kidnaper's hangout and charge it with artillery, to find—a love-nest."

Tina tossed her head.

"I think it's disgusting. Everybody thought the schoolteacher was such a 'splendid young man; such a fine influence,' and all that."

"They found the license plates," said Wally.

"Yes. And they found someone who thought he saw a black automobile. I guess that's the bag."

Matter seemed perfectly cheerful about it, but Wally felt as though he ought to apologize for the way the thing had fizzled out.

"Suppose you take me home, Wally," said Tina. "Mother went in to the hospital with this Mrs. Goggin. It's cooler at home on the porch than it is out here."

Wally was glad of the suggestion.

"Come along, then," he said. "But I think we'll just go round by way of the Spring for a last checkup, if you don't mind."

"Of course I don't mind," said Tina. She was a very agreeable girl.

Matter waved to them as they drove away.

It was late afternoon when they reached the Spring. People were beginning to pack up to go home. Mrs. Forsythe had just scored game and rubber on a bid of five hearts doubled and redoubled. Six men were unloading a melodeon from a truck, for the afternoon church service, and the young people were wondering whether, after the service was over, it wouldn't be all right to start a dance in the pavilion.

The parking space was still crowded with cars, but a few of the early-comers had pulled out and Wally managed to find a vacant space for his flivver. He was busy backing and cutting to get in when Tina gave a little cry and caught his arm.

"Look!" she said. "Over there—that's Mr. Breen's car!"

Wally looked.

"Why, it can't be, Tina," he said. "It's got only one spare wheel and no motor-meter radiator cap, and it has Missouri license plates. It's the same size and make of car—that's what fooled you."

"It's Mr. Breen's car," she insisted. "I know it is."

"How can you say that when it hasn't any of the marks?"

"How would you recognize a person you knew, even if he shaved off a mustache or something? That car's stood right across the street from our house thousands of times. I tell you, it's Mr. Breen's car."

"Well, come along. We'll have a look at it."

Wally had no confidence in her identification. The "murder car," as Will Breen's black Buick had come to be called, simply could not be standing there in the parking space just like that, with all the other cars. But one had to humor a girl.

The car was securely locked. They walked around the car peering in through the windows, but could make out nothing unusual. A light lap robe trailed carelessly from the back seat on the floor.

"Recognize the lap robe?" asked Wally.

"Mr. Breen had one like that, I think," the girl said uncertainly. "But look here, Wally, there's no radiator cap at all, and see this license plate—it isn't screwed on, just set there on the bracket."

"By George! You're right." A shiver ran over him. "Wait. I've got the engine number."

He dug a crumpled "instruction sheet" from his pocket. The number checked.

"Listen," he said. "You go and call the sheriff and get him out here. I'm going to stay right here to see nobody touches this thing. If you happen to see Jeffers around, tell him and get him here. Don't tell anybody else. Don't let them hear what you say on the telephone."

The girl hesitated. She was very pale. She trembled a little.

"If you'd rather, I'll go," said Wally. "And you stay here."

"Oh, no! I'd rather go. Of course one of us has to stay. I'm all right. I won't tell anybody."

He watched her weave her way in and out among the parked cars and disappear in the direction of the recreation center where there was a telephone in the vestibule of the dance pavilion.

The air was soft and golden, and tasted of dust and green things, of gasoline, heat. From a distance came the faint wheeze of the melodeon, and in growing volume the sound of voices in an old hymn. Wally sat down on the running board of the car. He noticed two little spots of what might have been red paint, but wasn't. Tina! Could you beat her? Hundreds of people had seen that car standing there, and its flimsy disguise had fooled them all but her. Fooled him, and he had seen that car of Will Breen's hundreds of times.

A man came and backed his car out of the huddle. He looked curiously at Wally, but said nothing.

Twenty minutes. Twenty-five. The sheriff ought to be getting here. There he was with Tim and another deputy. Tina was with them, pointing out the way.

# CHAPTER 25

THE SHERIFF LOOKED old and gray and weary.

"You're sure, Wally?" he asked.

"Certain, Sheriff. I checked the engine number. It was Tina Johnson that spotted it."

"Been standing right here all the time, looks like," said Tim, who had been inspecting the tire marks. "Look, these tracks left by them fellows that come in here today's a whole lot fresher."

"We'd better tow it uptown," said the sheriff. "Too many people around here. Is the brake on, Tim? Well, get the door open. Smash the glass, I guess. Reach in and let off the brake. Use your handkerchief. May be a fingerprint on that brake-knob."

Someone, of course, had seen the sheriff's arrival and already the crowd was collecting. "Stand back, now, everybody."

They made a solid wall—men and boys mostly, a few women. One woman began to weep loudly; a girl giggled and said, "Quit your pushing." In the distance the melodeon wheezed "Nearer, my God, to Thee." A blue jay perched on a branch overhead flirted his tail and squawked a protest.

"Look out for those license plates—they're not screwed on."

They fell off as the car was moved and Tim picked them up carefully, with his handkerchief, and put them in the back of the sheriff's car.

"I could drive her in, Sheriff," he said. "The wheel's been wiped clean. We won't find no fingerprints."

"All right," the sheriff agreed. "You, Wally, come along. The young lady doesn't have to come. The rest of you folks stay right here. There won't be a thing for you to see or hear if you come up to town."

"I want to go with you, Wally," said Tina. She was clinging to his arm. "I want—to go home. It's really pretty horrible. I guess I haven't any imagination; I never just realized till now that he's been—killed."

"Come on, fellers," said somebody in the crowd. "If the car was here, likely he's here too. Let's have another good look all through these bushes and up there under the hill."

"No reason to think, just because the car's here they planted him here," objected a deep voice. "More likely the other way, matter of fact."

The crowd, however, began to disperse, and boys and men like a pack of beagles began hunting through the brush, each hoping he might be the lucky one. In the distance, a weak little human voice, like a radio turned too low, was upraised in the wailing intonation of prayer.

The sheriff called his second deputy and directed him to stay and keep the crowd from following to town.

"Coming with me, Wally?" he asked.

"No, sir. I've got my bus here, and Tina wants to go home."

So the procession started, the sheriff in the lead, next, the black sedan with Tim at the wheel, Wally's flivver last.

"I don't see how he can bear to sit there in that car and drive," said Tina, with her eyes on the car ahead.

"All in the day's work for Tim," said Wally. "I'm going to drive 'round by the grove and pick up Matter. He'll want to be in on this."

"I used to think," said Tina, "that it would be wonderful to be a detective. I won't ever think that again."

She gave a little sigh of relief as they turned off toward the grove and the back of the black sedan was no longer before her eyes.

"You'd make a good one," said Wally. "You know what

you are seeing when you look at it. But it is pretty dismal. Seeing that car kind of got me, too. Till then it had been all kind of like a story. That made it seem real."

They were both badly shaken. Matter's enthusiasm over the news was a help. Jones, of the Chicago *Record-Herald,* and his attendant camera man had drifted in at the grove, and the three newspapermen had been, Wally suspected, holding a palaver on the dud that the Keedora mystery had turned out to be. They all got aboard the flivver—Jones in the seat with Wally and the girl, the other two on the running boards—and made such speed as the old car had in her on the way to town.

"Listen," said Wally to the girl; "we've got to get to the sheriff's office right away. You drive on home in the car. I'll be up at your house later and tell you what they find."

"All right," she said simply.

She was that kind of girl—never making objections or offering suggestions.

When they reached the county building, the sheriff had just arrived, and Tim was driving the black sedan into the enclosed yard back of the building. The sheriff was not best pleased to see the newspapermen, but he made no objections to admitting them and even stood beside the "murder car" while a picture was taken.

The examination of the car was careful and complete, and took a long time; but it was barren of results. A few blurry fingerprints were found, but these might as well have been the prints of William Breen himself as of anybody else. They were so vague as to be useless. The back of the car was deeply stained with blood, but this meant nothing new, as all were already convinced that the missing banker had met with foul play. The license plates? As a clue they proved worthless. A check with Missouri authorities by telephone showed that these plates had been issued to a certain Charles Gibson, of St. Louis, the year before. The St. Louis police reported that Charles Gibson, a carpenter by trade, reputation excellent, had removed permanently with his family. It was said he had been offered a job somewhere in Iowa.

Charles Gibson was found right in Keedora, living with his wife and four children in a cottage on Linden Street. He was, he said, foreman at the sash and blind factory. Yes, those were his old license plates. He recalled that a month or so earlier, soon after he came to Keedora, he and his family had spent a Saturday afternoon at the Spring. He had stopped by at the post office on the way to the Spring and had found his new Iowa plates in the mail. He had removed the old plates and put on the new ones there in the parking space at the Spring. Must have left the plates right there where he took them off. No suspicion attached to him.

Searchers at the Spring found the missing motor-meter and the second spare wheel belonging to the black sedan, more or less hidden in the bushes, and brought them in. On the motor-meter was found an indistinct fingerprint that might possibly check with the one found on the empty shell that the sheriff had picked up at the scene of the crime. Probably the same hand had thrown both objects away—but what did that get anybody?

"Might fingerprint everybody in Keedora and Deland," Matter suggested helpfully. "But of course you won't. People don't like to have their fingerprints taken, for some reason. And even if you did it, you might draw a blank. This killer, this elusive Mr. K., might be somebody from almost anywhere. Can't fingerprint everybody that ever came to Keedora."

The sheriff said nothing. He had, however, his own ideas. If the black car seen by the old moonshiner at the limekiln was actually the "murder car"—and the sheriff was inclined to believe it was—then the murderer was almost certainly someone living in Keedora. It was very unlikely that a stranger would have found that carefully hidden track up the gulch.

And more: the man who thought of that spot as a place of concealment was almost certainly not one of the younger generation that had been growing up for the last fifteen years. In the day of "bicycle runs" the old limekiln—a ruin even then—had been a favorite objective. It was supposed to be picturesque and romantic. People snapped kodaks at it, and Myrtle Frink, who was an artist, though she had never taken a lesson, made a painting of it that looked something like an explosion in an ink factory and took a blue ribbon at the State Fair.

The man who pushed the black Buick up that overgrown road had probably been one of the young beaus of that forgotten time—a man, say, of fifty or so. Plenty of men of that age in Keedora, of course. Will Breen's own age. Who among them had reason to hate the banker? Plenty, probably, but it narrowed the thing down.

Of course, in the continued absence of the "corpus delicti," nothing much could be done, but there was the fingerprint. The sheriff put the empty shell and the motor-meter carefully in the safe. He must try and get that man Jeffers to let him take his prints. He hoped earnestly that they would not check.

CHAPTER 26

NORMAN JEFFERS had put in a hard day. In his battered roadster he had visited all fronts of the big search, and had been on hand for most of the major events—the finding of the license plates, the rescue of Chester Dawes from the well, the near-riot at the Hastings farm where Old Man Hastings had resented the intrusion of the searchers and had been inclined to stand on his rights, a shotgun in hand.

He had settled a dispute over territory between two rival squads that had got their maps mixed. He had supplied two stranded cars with gasoline and pulled a third out of a ditch. He had taken two mild cases of sunstroke up to the hospital in town and had returned a straying infant to the arms of its hysterical mother. It was late afternoon when he reached the Spring on his last round.

The long tables were still loaded with food, and people still sat along the benches in groups, still eating. The big ice-cream freezers standing under a tree were guarded by a severe woman armed with a long spoon, who was holding off with difficulty the usual swarm of small boys that always gathers about a parked ice-cream freezer as fruit flies gather to a basket of grapes.

The horseshoe pitching contest was entering the finals—a silence, a ringing metallic plunk, a shout.

From farther up the grove, where the religious services were about to begin, came a preliminary wheeze from the cottage organ.

To Matter it would have seemed a humorous scene, deriving as it did from tragedy. It did not seem humorous to Jeffers. The whole thing had gone flat and distasteful, like a half-empty bottle of beer left standing in the sun.

Women offered him sandwiches; others pressed upon

him oozy pieces of pie, dripping fruit juice. The woman with the spoon brushed aside the clustering small boys and dug a dollop of pink ice cream for him out of the depths of one of the freezers. But the sight and smell of the food sickened him. It was not food that his body was demanding. With a muttered excuse he hurried away.

"Did Miss Marsh find you, Mr. Jeffers? someone called after him. "She was here just now, asking for you."

Flora Marsh! Why couldn't she leave him alone? His one idea was escape. He found a footpath leading into the friendly shelter of the grove and made his way along it, away from the tables and the people. But at a turn of the path he came full upon Flora Marsh. She was sitting on a dead tree trunk with a sheaf of wilting wildflowers lying across her knees. He wanted to turn and run, but she had seen him.

"Norman!" she cried; "I'm so glad you've come. I've got to talk to you."

"Listen, Flora," he said coldly. "There isn't anything for you and me to talk about. We're all washed up. I wish you'd get that straight."

He turned to go.

But she caught him by the arm and clung to him.

"I can't let it be that way," she said. "Not now—after I've seen you again. We loved each other once. There's still something between us. It will always be there. I've been very unhappy, and I can see you have been unhappy, too. We need each other. Can't we—not go back, for the past is dead—but go on?"

He felt how she was trembling and saw that her eyes were filled with tears. Women, he thought, are the very Devil for persistence. You have to hit them with a club.

"I didn't intend to tell you—about myself," he said grimly. "You won't like it; but you asked for it."

He worked with nervous fingers at the cuff of his left

sleeve, stripped back the linen and held out his arm for her to see.

She looked at the thin arm, scarred with innumerable little blue pits and a few angry red splotches. A little cry escaped her.

"Well," he said, "that's that." He rolled down his sleeve again and buttoned the cuff. "I'll be getting along now, Flora. Good-by—for good this time."

"Norman, look at me!"

He had kept his eyes away from her face. He looked at her, and what he saw in her face was neither pity nor disgust, but love and understanding.

"It's not 'good-bye,' " she said. "Don't you understand, Norman? I love you."

She drew him gently toward the mossy tree trunk where she had been sitting when he came along, and they sat there, side by side— the man stooped over, staring ahead unseeing into the thicket, she with her arms around him.

"I think you must be crazy, Flora," he said at last. "What do you want of me? I'm no good. I'm a hophead, and I wash other people's cars for a living. What is there in that for you? Don't count on 'reforming' me. Probably it's too late. Probably it can't be done."

"I'm not going to preach, Norman," she said. "I have no right—after the way I failed you—to ask you to do anything for my sake. All I want is to give you my love."

"All right," he said shortly.

He thrust a hand into a secret inner pocket and drew out a little leather case. For a long minute he sat, holding it in his hand.

"You wouldn't think a man could hesitate," he said, with a hard laugh, "between a home, decent living, love—and this! But even now I'm calling myself a fool for thinking I can give it up. It's going to mean a trip through hell. A thousand times easier to go up against the Boche guns than to do this."

He drew back his arm and flung the case away, as far as he could, into the tangle of undergrowth. He turned toward her then, and took her into his arms.

Intent on their own drama, neither had heard the commotion on the picnic grounds that resulted from the finding of the black sedan. They did not hear, either, unless subconsciously, the strains of the melodeon leading the chorus of voices through the heart-comforting melody of "Nearer, my God, to Thee." It was their supreme moment, and they were alone together in a world where other people and their unimportant reactions had ceased to exist.

The little knot of men who broke through the brush in the ardor of the renewed corpse-hunt saw two quite ordinary middle-aged persons rather ridiculously clasped in each other's arms. Stifling their sniggers and bawdy comments till they should be out of earshot, the searchers crossed the path and disappeared up the wood.

"It seems strange, doesn't it, Norman, that we have been living all these years in the same place without meeting each other, and that it should be poor Mr. Breen who has brought us together?"

"Perhaps Saint Peter will chalk it up on the credit side for him," said Jeffers. "The old devil is going to need all the credits he can muster in the place where he's gone. Wouldn't be surprised if he has done more good to others by disappearing than by anything else he ever did."

"Don't be so bitter," Miss Flora said gently. "He's dead, I suppose."

" 'De mortuis—' eh? Well, if you like, we'll come out here every year and hang a wreath on this old log in his memory. How would that be?" he laughed with tender indulgence.

Miss Flora picked up her bouquet of wildflowers from the ground where she had dropped them, and began plaiting a wreath. "Get me some more flowers, Norman—this kind, with the long stems—"

When they went away presently, arm in arm down the path, the completed wreath lay on the log where they had been sitting. Very appropriately, too, as it happened. Someone coming down the path a little later saw it there, and it gave him a momentary shock. But no; the soft earth under the old log had not been disturbed anew. It still held its grisly secret. Miss Flora never knew that if she had poked a little harder with the ferrule of her parasol, at the spot where its little round impression could be seen, it would have encountered a Panama hat, and under that a cold face where the worms were already at work. "Macabre," Wally Price would have called it.

But Nature has no sense of humor. She is like a thrifty housewife taking what she has and making of it what she can. She was busy now resolving William Breen back into his elements; so much salt, so much calcium. It would all be useful next spring for the factory of green leaves and grass she was running in that glen. In a different way she was using, too, all the contacts and excitements of Will Breen's tragedy, setting up new human reactions that would blossom into future events and keep the world moving. A time such as this, when everybody is boiled up together in a froth of emotion and excitement, is the time she seizes to produce some of her most striking effects. Nothing is wasted or thrown away in her economy.

CHAPTER 27

MILLY SLATER lay in a wheelchair out under the trees in the garden, and watched the dancing shadows of the leaves on the close-clipped lawn. She was not thinking. It was painful to think. The only way to be perfectly happy, she perceived, was to switch off thought as one turns off the irritating voice of the radio, and live like a plant or a bird, drinking in the beauty of the world. Bees were busy in the tall lilies against the wall; two yellow butterflies were chasing each other in a silly dance over the mignonette; a robin came out to enjoy the spray of the garden sprinkler, walking about in the miniature rain in short little rushes; a light breeze fluttered a lock of her soft hair against her cheek. She knew that presently she would have to think, but at the moment she was happy in the sensation of being alive, untroubled by memories or regrets or fears of the future.

It was Harold's step on the grass that broke the spell. She shut her eyes, trying to hold it fast a little longer. No use; it was gone.

Harold walked carefully, not to rouse her if she were asleep. He stood beside her chair. She felt him there, close to her, and was astonished to find that no thrill came to her with his nearness. Her heart did not hurry its even beat. She felt—nothing. He might have been just anybody, standing there. Slowly she opened her eyes.

"Milly," he said, "did I wake you?"

"I wasn't asleep."

He took one of her white, nerveless hands and held it in his. His voice shook with emotion.

"Gee!" he said, "it's good to see you out again. You'll soon be well."

"Yes. I'll soon be well." He missed the note of reluctance

in her voice. "Why, Harold, what have you been doing? These blue and red splotches on your hands—Painting something?"

"I scrubbed with sand soap, but it won't all come off. You remember that old iron hitching post up in our attic? The one shaped like a nigger* boy holding a ring? We used to make up games about him when we were kids. Well, nothing would suit Grandma but to have him out again, set up where he used to be in front of the house. She wanted him all painted up again the way he used to be—red shirt and blue pants. I've been doing it. I can tell you everybody that comes along the street takes a good stare. Wally Price says he's going to do a piece about him for the paper."

"How is your grandmother?"

"Oh, she's fine. We've moved her back into the front bedroom. Uncle Will's room. She wanted it—I don't know why. I thought you wouldn't mind, Milly."

"What would I have to say about it?"

"Why, I mean—" He blushed all over his open, boyish face, up to the roots of his blond hair." When we are married, you know. It's the biggest bedroom, of course, but I thought—"

"Harold," she said gently, "we aren't ever going to be married."

"Why, Milly! Not right away, of course, if you don't want. But there's no reason, now—Grandma wants us to be married. She always has. She was talking about it just this morning. I—You—" He was incoherent, jarred out of himself. "You don't mean what you said, Milly."

"I do mean it," she answered. "Don't you see, Harold, everything is all different. I'm different. I've—been dead. I'm not the same person I was. I don't just know how to put it in words, but it's true. I won't ever be the same person

---

*We thought hard about this word and decided to leave Mary Atwater's original language.   —ed.

again."

"Milly! Don't you—love me any more?"

"No, Harold. You're sweet, and I don't want to hurt you, but I don't love you the way I did. Not like a lover."

"But—you're sick now. When you get better—when you're well again—"

She rocked her head against the pillow.

"Not ever again. I had to tell you." She shut her eyes to shut out the sight of his contorted face. It didn't seem fair to look at him when he was crying. "You have your grandmother to take care of, Harold. I've often thought that she makes more difference to you than I ever could. Some day it will be different. I'm just 'girl' to you—any girl. We were both so terribly young. I suppose you were just 'boy' to me. What do you know about me? What do I know about you—the real you, deep inside?"

She opened her eyes. He was standing beside her, a little turned away, not looking at her. She saw how slim and young and blond he was—just a boy. The man he was going to be—what would he be like? Impossible to say. She saw him impersonally, without emotion. He was a nice boy, but that was all. Strange to remember how he had filled her universe. Love was like a sickness, she saw— a touch of madness that made things for a time quite different from reality. A hummingbird was going along the row of petunias, hanging motionless in a blur of bright wings before each open bell of color in turn. A big white cat was sunning himself on the top of the wall.

"Everything is going to be all right, Harold," she said. "Everything *is* all right."

"How can you say that!" he cried, in a choked voice. "Everything's all wrong, if you won't marry me. After—after what we did—"

"I'm sorry for what we did," she said slowly. "I wish we hadn't."

"I wish we hadn't, too," said the boy. "But, gosh! it's pretty tough, being young. It wasn't as though we didn't intend to get married. Milly, don't you see that we've got to get married, now?"

"No," she said.

She wanted to say more, to explain to him just how she felt, but she could not find the words.

"I'll—go."

He dashed his paint-smeared hand across his eyes. She was not looking at him, just lying there staring at nothing. Peaceful. Why! she looked—happy! He turned and stumbled away through the shrubbery.

Milly shut her eyes and slept.

When she awoke she felt, before she saw, that Jim was sitting beside her and that the shadows were long on the grass.

"Jim," she said. She was glad to have him there. She held out her hand to him and he took it in his big palm. "It's lovely here in the garden," she said. "I've been asleep a long time. I feel wonderfully better."

"Did you mean what you told Harold?" the man asked gently. "Don't talk about it unless you want to."

"I meant it, Jim. I've been wanting to talk to you. I want to go away, Jim. Soon."

He sat silent for so long that she wondered whether he had heard her. "You'll have to help me, Jim—with Mother. I could go, I suppose, to some sort of 'convalescent home' up north somewhere for a while, till I get strong. I want to go alone."

"It would do you good to get away for a while," he said slowly. "Don't worry. We'll manage it somehow."

"I don't mean 'for a while,' Jim. I don't want to come back—ever."

"Why? " he asked.

She was not looking at him. She did not see the pain in

his face or hear it in his steady voice. She was not thinking about Jim.

"I'm a murderer, Jim," she said, in a voice hardly more than a whisper. "I'm as much a murderer as the man who killed Will Breen. Perhaps—I don't know—it's worse to kill a life that never had a chance to live at all than to kill somebody like Mr. Breen who had had his life, or most of it."

"But, child, you mustn't blame yourself that way!"

He clasped her hand so tight that his fingers bruised her.

"I don't 'blame myself,' " she said. "I don't understand my own feelings. I'm not—sorry. Living isn't much fun, Jim. I wouldn't hate anybody that took my life away from me. It isn't remorse I feel. I just feel—somehow shut out, cut off, as though I didn't 'belong' any more. I don't suppose you can understand."

"I—understand, all right," he said. "But don't you owe something to Harold, Milly?"

He did not add "to me." She owed him nothing, after all.

"I don't think so. He's just a boy. He'll be all right. But I've just got to get away where everything is—different. Perhaps if I do that, I can start over."

He raised her hand, that still lay in his, and pressed it against his cheek; then he laid it tenderly back in her lap and got to his feet. He stood over her, smiling down at her, and the comfort of his love and understanding seemed to flow over her. For some reason she felt like crying.

"You're—good, Jim," she murmured.

To her, as to Flora Marsh, it seemed that he was the best and kindest man in the world.

"As soon as you are a little stronger," he said. "Don't worry any more—about anything."

A few days later, in charge of a nurse, Milly was on her

way to a "health resort" in the north—out of the heat, away from the corn, the shrilling cicadas, the breathless nights; out of the life she had known, away from all the familiar faces, into a new life.

Jim Gordon, watching her train diminish up the track, knew that he had said good-bye to her forever. Oh, of course he would see her again some day. He would know that she was alive in the world. But she was gone from him—for always.

Mrs. Gordon wiped an easy tear out of the corner of her eye with a lacy handkerchief.

"Well, that was a good idea of yours, Jim," she said. "It is a trial to have a sick person in the house. Sick people are better off in a hospital or a sanatorium, I always say. I suppose you noticed how frazzled I was getting with the nursing and everything—though I didn't complain, did I?" She patted his arm. She was in one of her best moods. "It's still early, isn't it? Suppose we go down to the office for a while. That Marsh girl—though I suppose one really can't call her a 'girl' exactly—needs a lot more checking up than she gets from you. You're too easy on everybody, Jim—even too easy on yourself. But I suppose that's why I love you. Now that Milly's away I'll have more time. I can help you a little in the office. Really, I'd *like* to do it."

Jim made no answer. His heart was too full for words. He had not noticed what she said, but it did not matter. They got together into the car, parked behind the station, and drove off up the hill to town.

CHAPTER 28

WALLY PRICE AND MATTER, of the Kansas City *American*, sat together at a littered table in the dining room of the Keedora Hotel. Same heat, same smells, as on a night almost a week earlier; same strolling feet passing across the upper half of the open windows.

Wally felt terribly depressed. He had had such high hopes, based on the mystery of William Breen's disappearance, and now the thing had simply fizzled out. The mystery was as much a mystery as ever, but nobody was interested in it any more. Jones and his camera man had left right after the indeterminate ending of the great corpse-hunt. Of the big-time news hawks who had gathered in Keedora, only Matter remained.

Matter explained his loitering variously: he had nothing better to do; he had a vacation coming and might as well hang around Keedora as anywhere; he was writing a "piece"—magazine stuff—about the cost of crime. He showed Wally a battery of fat notebooks filled with figures and tables and a lot of writing in an odd, tiny hand, more like a woman's than a man's.

"The big Keedora murder mystery turned out a flop from the newspaper angle, all right," said Matter. "But don't take it to heart, youngster. After all, you didn't invent the crime and it isn't your fault it didn't click."

"I wish I knew what happened, and who killed him," said Wally crossly. At Matter's expression he asked, surprised, "Do you?"

"Of course," said Matter.

"Then—great God, man, what are we doing sitting here? Have you told the sheriff? Are you breaking the story in the morning papers?"

Matter shook his head.

"Nothing like that," he said. "The story's dead."

"Not if you know who did it!"

"Knowing and proving aren't the same thing, you know. The sheriff can't do anything. What has he got? A blood-stained automobile that belonged to Mr. William Breen; a revolver that has fired one shot—revolver also identified as the property of William Breen; a spade that may or may not have something to do with the affair. No 'corpus delicti.' No witness that's seen anything more to the point than two parked cars and a man bending over a jack, or an automobile without license plates on an unused road."

"There's an empty shell with a fingerprint," said Wally.

"Yes, there's a fingerprint. Whose? Might be Breen's for all anybody knows. And you can't make a murder out of a fingerprint without a corpse. Suppose this thing wasn't a murder at all. I, for one, don't believe it was. But even granting somebody was killed—who was killed? We know well enough it was Breen, but as far as the evidence goes Breen might have killed some 'person or persons unknown,' and have lit out for other parts. The gun was Breen's gun. Don't forget that. And it's pretty well proved that the empty shell was fired from that gun."

"But you say Breen was killed?"

"Of course it was Breen. Nobody else is missing from around here, for one thing. This was a local affair; the car on the old road to the limekiln shows that. No stranger would have found that road."

"And you say you know who did it! Who told you? How did you find out?"

"Lots of people told me. I got most of it, though, talking to an intelligent young lady one afternoon at Webster's Grove, while the rest of you ran around in the sun, falling down wells and breaking up love-nests."

"You mean—Tina?"

Wally was deeply hurt. To think that Tina—

Matter laughed.

"Don't get excited, feller. She didn't know she was telling me. She doesn't know she has the answer. You have it, yourself, I guess, though you're so close to all this business that you don't get the slant on it an outsider does."

Miss Brill at her little desk by the door rattled her papers. In a minute she would tell them it was time to leave. She wasn't interested in what they were saying, even if she could hear it, and wasn't even sorry she would be unable to get the conversation later from Etta. Etta had lost her job, and the new waitress was too busy making eyes at Oscar in the kitchen to be hanging around the table.

Matter lit one of his long cigarettes and inhaled deeply.

"The 'hidden drama' you were talking about, I suppose," said Wally.

"Exactly. The hidden drama. And talk about your heartbreak!"

Wally was surprised by his tone.

"I don't get it at all," said Wally peevishly.

He wished Matter would stop talking in riddles. It made him feel young and callow.

"Well, listen, youngster, here's how I dope it out: This William Breen stops beside the road to change a tire on his car. While he's stopped, a man comes along—a man who has, say, a big indignation in him; a man that's got an argument to make or a score to settle. Anyhow, a man Will Breen doesn't want to see and has, maybe, been avoiding. The man stops. That farmer, you remember, saw two cars parked beside the road. Breen can't get into his car and drive away because he hasn't got his wheel on yet, and he knows he's in for trouble, so he edges close to the front of the car where he's got this gun.

"There was an argument, we'll guess. It wasn't a holdup, because the money Breen had with him to close that deal over in Deland was all there when the car was found. This was something personal. Breen got excited and pulled the gun. Who got shot? It might have been the other fellow, but of course it was Breen. Shot with his own gun in a scuffle."

"Why! That wouldn't be murder at all!"

"That's what I've been telling you. Self-defense—manslaughter at the severest."

"Then why, if it was self-defense, didn't the man—the killer—come on into town and tell the sheriff what happened? He'd be in the clear. What would he want to go running around the country for, throwing license plates in the river, driving up old roads, digging a grave somewhere? It doesn't make sense."

"That's the interesting feature of the affair," said Matter. " Of course it's only guesswork—but suppose a third person was involved?"

"You mean there were two killers? I don't see how—"

"Oh, use your wits! I don't mean that there were two killers. Suppose the thing this man put up to Breen had to do with a third person. If the killer came in and told his story, this third person would suffer."

"You mean—a woman?"

"Perhaps. The old gag of 'cherchez la femme' isn't far off the truth, you know."

"But—Mr. Breen! You didn't know him. You never saw him. Like a time-clock. You couldn't imagine Mr. Breen mixed up with a woman."

To Wally the idea was fantastic.

"Well, anyway," said Matter, "there you have my guess. I have an idea it comes pretty close to the mark."

"But who was this killer?" insisted Wally.

"Perhaps it's just as well you shouldn't know," said Matter gravely. "It isn't newspaper stuff—take my word for that—any more than it's anything for the courts. I wouldn't think about it too much if I were you. It's finished. Forget about it."

"All right," said Wally, swallowing his disappointment. Privately he intended to get it out of Tina as soon as possible. "But just the same you're the most aggravating, irritating—" He gulped.

"Too bad you feel that way," said Matter, a twinkle in his eyes. "I suppose feeling like that—you wouldn't care to come to K.C. with me next week."

"What—do you mean?" stuttered Wally.

"Well, it's like this. I figured you sort of had something coming to you for all the work you've been doing on this thing, even if it did turn out a dud. I've kind of taken a fancy to you and that Tina of yours. You're an earnest worker. You'll make a good newspaperman some day. And that Tina girl—she's all yours, Wally, worse luck—is just the best specimen of the human female that I ever came across. You'd bring her along?"

"If you think I'd go half a mile away without her, you're crazy," said Wally.

"I'm a kind of privileged character in K.C.," Matter went on. "I asked my boss to make a job for you, and he says to bring you along."

"I don't know how to thank you. I—"

"That's all right, youngster—some day maybe you'll have the fun of giving some other cub a leg up in the game. But all things considered, your thanks ought to go to the 'late unlamented' Mr. William Breen."

"Funny," said Wally. "Mr. Breen never did anything for anybody in his life; but by getting himself killed he's done a lot for me, and for other people, too."

"You'd be surprised," said Matter. He took a notebook from his pocket and turned the leaves. "Of course I haven't talked to everybody in Keedora—extra gasoline sold, estimated about five thousand gallons; hot dogs, haven't got all the figures yet; merchandise, all kinds—rubber boots

that had been in stock ten years, cleaned out; romances—
hard to get accurate figures, but I know of ten. Did you
know that fellow Jeffers got married yesterday? Yes, to that
Miss Marsh in the real estate office. Mortgages renewed,
loans renewed. A new glue factory. Fact. Fellow at the hotel
told me about it. Intended to take his factory to Eldora and
even had a site under option. Came over here last Sunday
to see the excitement and that Chamber of Commerce
fellow got hold of him. Told me he signed papers this
morning with Gordon for a tract of land down by the
railroad. You know Gordon?"

Wally did not notice Matter's odd tone as he mentioned
Jim Gordon's name.

"Of course I know Mr. Gordon," he said. "Kind of a nice
guy, but one of those people—you know—that just lets
things happen. No fight in him. Never has anything to say
for himself."

" 'Still waters,' I suppose, and all that?"

"Well, I don't know. The kind you'd never notice in a
crowd, even if there were only three or four others."

Matter closed his notebook and put it back into his
pocket. "Funny thing," he said, "this is the first crime I've
checked that's all on the 'plus' side of the ledger. Everybody
wins—except Breen, of course, and the killer. A lot of
people, I wouldn't wonder, are better off dead than alive."
He did not say whether he meant William Breen or someone else. "Come on, let's get out of here before we're
thrown out."

He dropped the paper tube of his burnt-out cigarette
into his coffee cup and rose. . . .

The killer? Poor soul! He would have been happier dead
than living, no doubt. If he had been given to dramatizing
himself, he would have gone out to Catamount Spring and,
sitting on the log where Flora Marsh's withered wreath still
lay, would have put a bullet through his head. But he had

no sense of drama. His weary life goes on much as before, though empty now of everything that gave it beauty and meaning. Perhaps he thinks that perhaps—some day—It is hard to eradicate all hope from the human soul. Perhaps he does not know how wretched he is.